Alice May Quinn

Sweet Astreanere and Other Poems

Alice May Quinn

Sweet Astreanere and Other Poems

ISBN/EAN: 9783744711845

Printed in Europe, USA, Canada, Australia, Japan

Cover: Foto ©Andreas Hilbeck / pixelio.de

More available books at **www.hansebooks.com**

Sweet Astreanere

AND

OTHER POEMS.

BY

ALICE MAY QUINN,

OF

CONNERSVILLE, IND.

———•o•o•o•o•———

CINCINNATI:

ELM STREET PRINTING COMPANY, 176 AND 178 ELM STREET

1872.

CONTENTS.

CONTENTS.

IN MEMORIAM.

AUTHOR'S PREFACE.

I.

My little book thou art complete,
  Dear treasure of my youthful heart,
With soulful thought thou art replete,
  For of my soul thou formest a part.
Thy pages teem with fancies wild,
  They seem to blush, to smile, to weep;
Now merry as a romping child,
  Now grave to sadness most unmeet.

II.

Thou dost portray my every mood:
  Sad, thoughtless, tender, reckless, glad,
Bright mirror of my maidenhood.
  Oh if thy pages never had
Been written by my eager pen,
  What would have been my fate to-day?
Where would those thoughts vanish then?
  Say, Clio, could they pass away

III.

From me and leave no trace to tell
  That in my soul they had their birth?
And tell me now that here they dwell,
  Oh will they linger long on earth?
No answer, proud imperious muse.
  Well, since of me thou seemest tired,
Go back to Helicon, infuse
  Thy fires to others less inspired.

(5)

IV.

And now, my book, my fond beloved,
  Forth on a mission thou art sent;
Go to the world of workers, prove
  That 'tis *no task* to be content.
Go tell the maiden in her cot,
  Where she was born and gently bred,
That love and peace alas are not
  Accorded to the highly wed.

V.

Go tell the peasant that his king,
  Despite his wealth, his crown of gold,
Is subject to deep suffering,
  Victim of death and treachery bold.
Go tell the youth athirst for fame,
  Athirst for war's red honors bright,
That when he wins a deathless name.
  Death may his earthly GLORIES BLIGHT.

VI.

Go out into the critic's world,
  With all thy faults, thine errors too,
Display thy flag, so proud unfurled,
  Bearing this motto, *Ever true I fain would be.*
But if I err, the blame lies with untutored youth,
  Who loves romance—strange, rich and rare—
The which I found in sober truth.

IV.

Go tell the world that naught but God,
  Can guide us to the land of bliss,
That those who murmur 'neath His rod,
  Can never deem their spirits His.
Go forth and bring me my reward,
  Man's blessings, boundless that on high,
Will wait the coming of the bard,
  And friendships that can never die.

Dedication Address to Old Fayette

I.

FAYETTE! of thee my muse now joyous sings,
Forth in thy praise her voice exultant rings,
Fresh as the songs of silver-throated birds,
That in the dawning springtime erstly stirs
The dreamer's soul with joy, and proud inspires
His heart with music for his magic lyre.
For, Fayette, long hast thou well guarded me,
Home of adoption since from o'er the sea,
An infant stranger in my father's arms
I came, unconscious of life's raging storms,
To dwell secure within thy sheltering breast,
Adopted daughter of the smiling West.

II.

Alone, unknown and friendless, came we o'er
The briny deep to bright Columbia's shore,
Seeking protection 'neath the banner's wave,
Unfurled in glory o'er monarchy's grave.
When on Britannia's shores my father stood,
Breathing farewell to friends loving and good,
His brave heart failed him, and a burning tear
Told that his soul was stranger now to cheer.
Before him lay the ocean deep and wide,

Behind, Britannia in her power and pride,
On sea, the starry flag inviting waved,
On land, the red cross drooped o'er many a grave
Where martyred heroes slain in youth's first prime
In silence slumber, sons of fame sublime.
Who, for thee, Albion, gave their glorious lives,
Nor quailed when leaving kindred, home and wives.
My father stood o'erwhelmed in deeps of woe,
Oh, could he thus from all he cherished go,
Leave parents, brothers, sisters, kindred, all?
He back recoils, then hears his daughter call;
'Tis for her sake he clasped her to his breast
And turned once more toward the smiling West.

III.

O England, dark as are thy by-gone years,
I love thee still; with Cowper fall my tears
That lands as fair as thou should sullied be,
By such a stain as cruel monarchy.
I love Columbia's freedom, all her laws
Are bound together in that freedom's cause.
Nor kings, nor tyrants e'er o'er her can rule,
Of independence proud unrivaled school;
Yet, England, at that name my bosom thrills,
With longings wild my warm young heart fills,
To breathe again my far-off natal air,
And tread across her meadows green and fair;.
To catch the English lark's inspiring song,
And all her ancient ruins roam among;
To stand where Scott the Wizard of the North,
His lays entrancing poured in rapture forth;
Where Byron, Liberty's adoring son,
Immortal laurels for his genius won;

Where Milton sung heroic tales sublime,
And Cowper lauded nature's every clime;
Where Moore soul-thrill ng melodies composed,
Each one a gem that still resplendent glows.
'Tis said that Greece is poetry's natal home;
If so, like me far from her isle she roams,
Nor longer basks beneath the beauteous skies,
Where proud Olympus crowned with rainbows rise.
O'er England's heath, o'er Scotia's every hill,
And Erin's lawns, the Muses range at will;
Forgot by them the far-off lovely isles,
Where nature bland assumes her brightest smiles,
And now where kingdoms three unite in one,
Is heard the minstrel's lone inspiring song.

IV.

Much as I love the broad and smiling West,
The star-lit symbol of its freedom blest,
Still, still, my English heart doth cling to thee,
Adorin: Albion, princess of the sea.
As a tender mother loves an erring son,
When o'er Him crime a mantle black has flung,
Deserted by the friends that were his boast,
Which, if wealth graced him, were a countless host;
Now they condemn, nor mercy wish to show,
But to his doom doth long to see him go;
Despairing, bowed beneath a world's deep hate,
That mother near her hapless son doth wait.
Her breast sustains the wretch's drooping head,
And when afar the angel's hope has fled,
She soothes his anguish, nor her labor fails,
Just as she soothed once his infant wails.
Thus England, do I love and cling to thee,

E'en while I weep that direful monarchy
Doth crush thy ch'ldren 'neath his *ir n* heel,
Or hush their cries for liberty with steel;
Stifling their prayers in life's rich surging blood,
Or drives them homeless o'er the raging flood.

V.

Homeless? Ah! no, beyond Atlantic's tide
Proud stands Columbia, heaven-born freedom's bride;
With open arms the peerless beauty waits
To welcome them unto her lovely States,
And clasps them to her heaving bosom warm
To shield them from all future frowning harm.

VI.

Fayette, it was within thy shelt'ring breast
That first my father tasted freedom blest;
Within thy confines bright he learned with awe
To love the goddess, Liberty, each law
Made by the wise men of the Western World,
Who erst the eagle's flag proudly unfurled.
There, too, his English daughter learned to read
Of independence, that most sacred creed
Which lifts man God like high o'er earthly fears,
And wafts his soul toward the heavenly spheres.
'Twas there she shook the bondage from her soul,
Of bigotry, that millions doth control;
Dark curse of nations, cursed by kingly rule,
Of treason anarchy the ready tool,
And superstition, torturer of the mind,
'Neath whose iron hands low dying lie confined
The best impulses of heroic hearts
That dread naught mortal, yet at shadows start.

To sing her lyrics with untrammeled mind,
And leave her name with Fayette's fame behind,
Is the fond dream of her aspiring soul,
In fancy free to rove from pole to pole.

VII.

Fayette, thy daughter of adoption now,
Will wreath her blossoms wild around thy brow,
Nor fail to love and loyal reverence thee
For sixteen years the dearest home to me.
Wast not thou who gave her all she boasts,
True friends, a home, advantages a host;
Within thy schools her youthful hungry mind
Expanded, showing that therein confined
The gift of poesy unnoticed dwelt ;
Nor was it by its owner ever felt
Till thou, wise friend of struggling genius, told
Me that in time the bud would soft unfold,
Displaying all its wondrous beauty bright
In tints as varied, rich as rainbow light,
That fills with joy the dreamer. Oft I cry
For the rare gift of heaven-born poesy:
O God, I thank thee from my inmost soul.
To praise thee then shall be my Muses' role,
And from the prison freed
These very Muses honored John S. Ried.

VIII.

Another friend I must remember now,
One who has cheered my labor. On his brow
Is graved the stamp of kindness, deep true
The zeal that marks his earnest labor, too.
He toils untiring for untutored youth,

Instilling in each heart a love of truth;
His noble works above shall brightly glow,
His crown of fame, Professor Rippitoe.
More friends abundant, had I space
To mention, might this grateful passage grace;
But now, suffice it for me here to say,
That none's forgotten by me night or day.
Where fate may cast them evermore along,
With me they'll share my tender pulsing heart,
Nor from my memory shall no dear friend part.

IX

And thou, fair city, my dear erstly home,
In which I dwelt when o'er the sea I came,
I loving dedicate this book to thee;
Oh may it with thee live when I'm no more,
Yes, when I've crossed life's mystical shore.
I love the woods and vales and meadows green,
That near thy confines beautiful are seen;
Each silvery stream, each verdant sloping hill,
Rare beauteous zones of lovely Connersville.

Sweet Astreanere.

I.

WHAT is true love? is it a thing
  That man can at his pleasure buy,
Like lands or goods or costly ring
  That oft like shadows from him fly?
Or is't perchance a fleeting myth,
  A fancy empty as the air,
That fans the dreamer's cheek as with
  The fragrant breath of flowrets rare?

II.

Nay, 'tis a passion deep and true,
  Born in the heart that knows not guile;
A passion pure as virgin dew
  That gems the rosebud like the smile
Of seraph spirits from above,
  Which fancy paints in flowers to dwell.
Eternal, deathless is true love,
  It comes but once I know full well.

III.

And if, perchance, the cynic smiles
  In contempt at this beau ideal
Theory, held of human love

(13)

By poets that can never feel
Aught but the promptings of the soul,
  Which make or mar them, they obey.
To wear the mask is not the role
  Of poets e'en in this cold day.

IV.

Then let him list to this the tale
  Told by tradition, of the fate
Of two young lovers, dark the weal
  That marks a woman's jealous hate;
And while he lists let pity's tears
  Fall gently o'er each hallowed grave,
Where long hath slept, devoid of fears,
  Sweet Astreanere and Glenwold brave.

V.

In Cornwall dwelt a feudal knight,
  The proudest lord that graced the reign
Of England's virgin mistress bright,
  Elizabeth.   The darkest stain
That sullies her strange, grand career,
  Forgetting fair-haired Essex' fate,
Is this, the death of Astreanere,
  And Glenwold, her brave-chosen mate.

VI.

Oh she was fair and she was young
  As spirit of a poet's song,
As blue and melting were her eyes,
  As violets reared in Paradise;
And 'neath the glory of her hair,
  That swept like vail of molten gold

Over her shoulders white and fair,
   As bust of some great goddess old,

VII.

There smiled a face of beauty bright,
   For which Venus might envy own;
And on her brow as lilies white,
   Diana's star in splendor shone;
While round her lips of coral hue
   There played a thousand witching smiles;
And in her voice, sweet as the coo
   Of doves, there lurked enchanting wiles.

VIII.

In her fair form, as graceful, light
   As fabled sylph or young gazelle,
Were seen such wondrous charms as might
   In houries of the Orient dwell.
What wonder then that such a maid
   As Montague's flower, should honored be
By love of knights of every grade,
   Or princes from beyond the sea.

IX.

Sweet Astreanere, the heiress sole
   Of Montague's towers, knew care nor woe,
Till from the Queen of Britain came
   The summons for Glenwold to go
Afar upon the stormy main,
   To battle with the foreign foe.
Against the royal power of Spain
   She sent her knights to level low.

X.

The pride of him who held aloof
    From her religion and its rites.
She chose Glenwold with Essex fair,
    And Raleigh, bravest of her knights,
To fall upon the Spanish fleet,
    Capture the treasure galleys great,
That they might at her royal feet,
    With reverence lay the golden freight.

XI.

But was this thirst for power and wealth
    The queen's sole passion on that day,
When those three fearless knights she sent
    To forage on the briny sea?
Ah! no, the queen of kingdoms three,
    The virgin princess bowed to love,
On Glenwold she her heart bestowed,
    To keep him from his Cornish dove.

XII.

To separate the plighted pair,
    And hold the heart in stern restraint,
That proudly spurned her royal care,
    Was what the willful lady meant.
And when Glenwold the call received,
    That doomed him from his pearl to roam,
He sought sweet Astreanere one eve
    Ere parting from his Cornish home.

XIII.

It was the hour when flaming Sol
    No longer ruled the heavenly sphere;

And Luna, mistress of the night,
  Shed forth her silv'ry luster clear ;
As seated on her gleaming car,
  She op'ed her wild, nocturnal race,
Attended by a million stars,
  That hung like lamps of gold in space,

XIV.

That Astreanere, the Cornish rose,
  Pride of her haughty father's heart,
Sought out the bower that brightly glowed
  With floral jewels. Sad to part
With young Glenwold, the noblest knight
  That ever wore the avenging blade ;
Which swiftly flashed athwarth the light,
  A foe to vanquish, friend to save.

XV.

With loving heart the maiden sought
  The trysting place to her most dear,
And as she sat aneath the bower,
  Her eyes of azure shed a tear.
This meeting was to be their last,
  For months Glenwold would rove the sea,
Alone, within her father's towers
  Sweet Astreanere would mourning be.

XVI.

Athwarth the star-bejeweled sky
  The maiden's eyes cerulean roved,
As if, perchance, she might descry
  There scribed the fate of her beloved.

2

The bright lake, like a silver sea,
   Shone 'neath the young moon's crescent bea;
While near and far on hill and lea
   The ghostly shadows wanly gleamed.

XVII.

The night-bird, silent by his mate,
   Forgot to trill his sweet love-song ;
And from the depths of lonesome glade
   The owl's fell hoot was borne along.
The perfumed breezes fanned the cheek
   Of Astreanere, as 'neath the bower
She wailing sat 'mid blossoms sweet,
   Toying with Cupid's chosen flower.

XVIII.

The moments fled: a quivering sigh
   Went fluttering from the maiden's heart,
And to her tender love-lit eyes
   The tell-tale tears again would start.
But hark! what sound the stillness breaks?
   'Tis naught but warrior's fearless tread
That rings along the stony walk
   That to the bower of trysting led.

XIX.

Nearer the step approaches, then
   A voice deep, rich and full of power
Calls: "Astreanere, light of my soul,
   Art thou within thy rose-clad bower?"
With fluttering breath and blushing cheek
   Sweet Astreanere softly replies :

"Aye, Glenwold, thine own love is here,
  Of Montague's heart the treasured pride.

XX.

" But what hath caused thy coming late,
  What kept thee from thy dove to-night?
Surely no duty how'er great
  Could tempt thee from thy trysting plight."
"Sweet Astreanere," Glenwold replies,
  " Thy sire's behest must I obey ;
To-night he sought me out to learn
  The hour that I must needs away.

XXI.

"And while in converse I confessed
  To him my love for thee, sweet one,
Besought him soon to make us blest,
  A cloud of woe he cast upon
My heart, when in reply he spoke,
  With fiery glance and stormy brow,
'Sooner than see my daughter wed,
  With thee, sir knight, I'd lay her low.

XXII.

" 'With this, her father's aged hand,
  Glenwold of Britain, lowly born,
I'd stretch her lifeless on the sand,
  Fair as she is in life's bright morn.
Cecil, the pride of England's court,
  Prime minister of England's queen,
Hath asked the hand of Astreanere,
  Most beauteous maid 'er by him seen.

XXIII.

" ' Elizabeth smiles on the suit
   Her Majesty to Cecil gave ;
A dower such as might in sooth
   Tempt Plutus from his treasure cave.
So, Glenwold, think no more to wed
   With Montague's peerless daughter now ;
For ere from battle thou'lt return,
   A ducal crown shall gem her brow.'

XXIV.

'And with these words thy father left
   Me to my fate.   Oh, Astreanere !
Must we thus part of hope bereft,
   Oppressed by wretched, taunting fear ? "
He paused, in silent woe he gazed
   Upon the mystic vault of night;
With black despair his brain was crazed,
   Dark loomed the future in his sight.

XXV.

Those holy stars by lovers prized,
   Hope, love and faith, by clouds were riven ;
And in its glory through the skies,
   The blood-red orb of war was driven.
Astreanere leaned upon his breast,
   Weeping in hopeless, speechless woe ;
With his strong love she had been blest,
   How could her father bid him go ?

XXVI.

With faltering voice at length she spoke:
   "Glenwold, my sire's decree is stern ;

Yet sooner than his curse invoke,
    To do his will I now must learn.
My love for thee can never die,
    Not though by Hymen's chains I'm bound;
Cecil may wed with Montague's pride,
    With coronet gay I may be crowned,

XXVII.

" Still, Glenwold, still I am thine own ;
    My heart, my soul's best love is given
To thee, whatever woe may come
    To crush me, thou'rt my earth's sole heaven."
She ceased, her woman's heart was full
    With bitter grief to further speak,
And Glenwold with perceptions dulled
    Was as a wailing infant weak.

XXVIII.

Neither of those doomed lovers heard
    The loud approach of mail-clad feet,
Until the voice of Montague's lord
    Destroyed their trance, bitter yet sweet.
The lord of Montague, stern and old,
    Upon them with grim anger glanced;
Erect stood Glenwood, firm and bold,
    As to the rose-bower he advanced.

XXIX.

" How now, young Glenwold, would'st thou war
    Upon thy master?" asked the lord;
" That thou hast dared to enter here ;
    If so draw forth thy ready sword,
And here, with none but Astreanere

To witness, I'll my vengeance wreak;
And teach thee, Montague's lord, to fear.
How say'st thou now? Ah! why not speak?"

XXX.

Deep scarlet flushed the knight's fair face;
Swift from its steel sheath flashed his blade,
Advancing to Montague a pace,
In clarion tones he proudly said:
"An hundred henchmen dost thou boast,
Yet will I war with thee this hour,
And all thy faithful mail-clad host,
Come, 'gainst me lead thy vaunted power.

XXXI.

"To breathe farewell to Astreanere,
I sought this rose-clad bower of love;
If thou would'st fight afar from here
The mettle of our blades we'll prove.
But this sweet spot is far too pure
For men to sully with fell strife;
But out on yonder level moor
I'll teach thee that my blood is rife

XXXII.

"To battle with the knight that dares
To brand me as one lowly born,
While life with me its vigor shares
I'll brook from none insult or scorn."
Thus face to face they scowling stood,
The lord of Montague and the knight,
Who ne'er before in angry mood
Challenged the noble forth to fight.

XXXIII.

With bosom full of bitter ire, he
  Bade Glenwold say his sad farewell,
And turned him from the scorching fire
  That from his eyes of midnight fell.
Against the author of this woe
  Montague's proud soul rebellious rose ;
Elizabeth must surely know
  That 'gainst her Glenwold's heart was closed.

XXXIV.

Lord Montague loved the noble youth,
  Right proud was he when first he learned
That Astreanere possessed the heart
  For which a queen in silence yearned ;
And oft he dreamt ot Montague's hall,
  With Glenwold as its noble lord,
And Astreanere his peerless bride
  Surrounded by their feudal horde.

XXXV.

But all his hopes were swept away
  When Britain's queen beheld the knight;
She loved him in her jealous way,
  And hated Astreanere the bright.
Far from the maiden's side to roam
  She doomed Glenwold ; relentless ire
Consumed her bosom when in gloom
  He sought from service to retire.

XXXVI.

With cruel words the maid she bade
  To wed with Cecil the deformed,

Or on the block lay low her head,
   All pleadings from Montague were scorned.
To make Glenwold his bitter foe,
   To break his darling's h art for aye,
Montague was forced, grim, deathless woe
   Seemed on his wretched soul to lie.

XXXVII.

Sweet Astreancre half fainting clung
   To Glenwold; bitterest anguish tore
Her heart; while daggers of deep woe
   Were pierced unto the inmost core;
While he, o'erwhelmed in black despair,
   Strove, madly strove, to rend h.m free
From those fair arms that held him there.
   Both stood in speechless misery.

XXXVIII.

At length in tones broken and low,
   He spoke that last, that dread farewell;
From her fond clasp his form he tore,
   Leaving her helpless where she fell.
Afar he fled; none but the strange,
   Lone spirits, wandering through the night,
Knew of the tempest wild that raged
   Within his breast during that flight.

XXXIX.

From all that to his soul was dear,
   While in her bower of beauty bright,
Astreancre mourned with sigh and tear,
   The absence of her lover-knight.
And thus those two fond, loving hearts,

Ne'er more on earth, in life to meet,
Parted upon that summer eve,
   Glenwold, and Astreanere the sweet.

XL.

'Twas on the last night of the year,
   That Montague's peerless heiress bright,
Was doomed to wed the hunchback peer,
   Of England's court the shining light.
Cecil, the cunning statesman, clad
   In robes bedecked with jewels rare;
Exulting in the thought and glad
   That his would be this treasure fair.

XLI.

Impatient waited for the hour
   Of midnight, that would fix the fate
Of Montague's tender drooping flower.
   With joyous heart, and soul elate,
He restless passed from place to place;
   Plotting against the favorite three
That now found favor in the grace
   Of his proud mistress, recklessly.

XLII.

Essex, the fair, in secret wooed
   And won a bride; young Raleigh, wild,
A maid of honor gently sued ;
   And Glenwold firm, yet nobly mild,
Remained as true to Astreanere,
   As ever knight to lady kept,
Despite temptations that bestrewed
   The path o'er which his life was swept.

XLIII.

Their ruin Cecil fiercely craved,
   Death to the gallant trio then
Was e'er his watchword; oft he raved
   In fury for the blood of men,
Who each believed himself the friend
   Of Cecil.   Glenwold, wronged young knight,
Dreamt not that he could e'n pretend
   Affections false, as mirage bright

XLIV.

That flashes fore the fevered eyes
   Of traveler on the sun-scorched plain,
When with fierce thirst he almost dies,
   And cruel heat boils every vein;
When naught but burning wastes of sand
   Extend before his aching sight,
Until the tortured brain expands,
   And reason totters from her height.

XLV.

Then far beyond the sandy sea,
   In all its rural beauty rare ; .
Where silver streams are flowing free,
   And wild birds fill the perfumed air
With melodies rich, wildly sweet,
   An emerald grove his vision greets.
He struggles bravely on, and soon
   Reaches the spot to find it gone.

XLVI.

So when with woe deeply oppressed,
   The knight sought out the false one,

Believing all that he professed,
   Nor deemed him liable to wrong
A friend, he asked the peer to yield
   Back Astreanere, the Cornish rose.
Cecil declared 'twas not his heart,
   But his proud queen that for him chose.

XLVII.

Thus while upon the stormy main,
   Fighting for their country brave;
Scattering wild fear through haughty Spain,
   Their traitor friend and titled slave,
Against them roused the deadly ire
   Of her who wooed them all by turns;
Within her heart kindled the fire
   That o'er love's ashes fiercely burns.

XLVIII.

And on this last night of the year,
   When mirthful guests throng Montague's hall,
The hapless knights in durance drear
   Were lodged   Unheeded was their call
For freedom. Cecil had his way;
   This night would make his joy-cup full;
All this strangely grand display
   Was made the bride's sad fears to lull.

XLIX.

The rose of Cornwall lonely sate,
   Surrounded by her ladies gay,
Within her flower-dressed hall of state,
   Watching the clouds of leaden-gray,
That through the bleak and wintry sky

Flew on before the stormy blast,
She silent prayed that she might die,
   Though of her race she was the last.

L.

Silent and hopelessly she waits,
   Like one that's doomed erelong to die;
With all her wealth and beauty great,
   She fain would from her sorrows fly.
No smile illumes her beauteous face;
Mournfully she views the scene
   Of revelry that's taking place,
And gloom o'erclouds her brow serene.

LI.

At length the fatal hour arrives,
   Lord Cecil seeks Montague's pride,
And leads her from her virgin bower;
   The richest, yet most wretched bride,
That ever spoke the formal vows
   Which bind two lives for weal or woe;
All helpless to grim fate she bows,
   Nor dreams to say her tyrants "no."

LII.

Within a chapel grim and hoar,
   Whose rugged walls rich ivy vails,
Assembled round the altar, o'er
   Which an hundred tapers' flames
Low droops the flower of Montague's hall;
   Lord Cecil holds her trembling hand,
Dead silence reigns like fates' dark pall,
   Over the guests that silent stand.

LIII.

The priest with grave and solemn face,
  Exhorts the twain to love and trust,
To live in holy, heavenly peace,
  Each to the other be e'er just;
And then he speaks to Astreanere :
  "Lady of Montague, watch and pray,
Shake from thy soul all doubting fear,
  Thy queen's behest with love obey.

LIV.

"Smile on thy lord, nor tremble more,
  Nor grieve that thou shouldst wedded be
With one who from thy natal shore
  Hath swept the stain of popery."
He paused, the hush still, death-like reigns,
  Sweet Astreanere essays to speak,
But mute her coral lips remains,
  And lower droops the maiden meek.

LV.

As lamb in clutch of famished wolf,
  Without a hope of life it lies,
In its own gore to be engulfed,
  Silent, complainingless, it dies.
Thus Montague's rare and tender flower,
  Resigned herself up to her fate,
Dreaming of that sweet rose-clad bower
  Where Glenwold told her oft elate,

LVI.

How much he loved his own sweet rose,
  Her, of his soul, unrivaled queen;

And then with dread her young heart froze,
    As gazed she on this weird scene;
Herself in robes of ghostly white,
    The guests with faces all agloom,
The uncertain, pale and flickering lights
    That 'lume the chapel like a tomb.

LVII.

The service slowly is begun;
    Cecil responds in clarion tones,
But Astreanere with silent tongue,
    All helpless in her anguish moans.
The frowning bridegroom sees the change
    As to the marble floor she sinks,
And knows his treasure's life is o'er,
    For death now at life's fountain drinks.

LVIII.

Slow from her lips a crimson tide,
    Her life's rich blood is welling now,
And Cecil clasps his fainting bride,
    No longer frowning is his brow.
But Montague's lord, o'erwhelmed in woe,
    With eye of fierce, despairing fire,
Seizes his child, in accents low
    He prays that she may not expire.

LIX.

In vain, the prayers were offered late,
    Fainter and fainter came her breath,
For she in life's bright morning hour,
    Became the bride of cruel death.
Hushing the pulsing of their hearts,

In silc it awe the guests await
The closing of this bridal sceue,
To breathe, all seemed to hesitate.

ˉLX.

Sweet Astreanere, with loving eyes,
    Gazed on her father's gloom-wrapt face,
And pointing to the stormy skies,
    Smiled brightly, as if heavenly grace
Aided the maiden thus to part
    With life and all its luring joys.
No grief disturbs her breaking heart;
    Montague's rare flower all *hopeful* DIES.

LXI.

No sound disturbs the awful hush
    Which death hath cast upon the group
Of silent guests that gath red near,
    To gaze upon the blossom crushed
By England's heartless, tyrant queen,
    To gratify a fleeting whim;
The love of Glenwold, fresh and green,
    Was what the *virgin* sought to win.

LXII.

The hour of midnight saw the close
    Of Astreanere's short, hapless life;
And from the floor Lord Montague rose,
    Wrestling with all his giant might   -
With fierce emotions that consumed
    His heart. Lord Cecil slowly turns
And meets the noble's blazing eyes
    That to his soul of treachery burns.

LXIII.

Upon their swords their hands are placed,
　　Black hatred rages in each breast;
When lo! a sound the stillness breaks,
　　A mail-clad knight with haste hard pressed,
Strides through the chapel's open door,
　　Up to the altar with firm step,
And then Montague he bows before;
　　Over the scene his dark eyes swept.

LXIV.

He lifts his visor from his face,
　　What do the startled peers behold?
The features fair, the form of grace,
　　That marks the knight Glenwold, the bold.
"Lord Montague," spoke the noble knight,
　　" To bid adieu to Astreanere,
Of Cornwall rare and beauteous light,
　　This gloom-wrapt hour I now am here.

LXV.

"Afar beyond the weltering wave,
　　Where sleeps the golden god of day,
I go with Raleigh true and brave,
　　To find a home where I may stay;
Untroubled by the strife for power,
　　Where kings and statesmen never rule;
But where during each sunny hour
　　I'll learn in nature's chosen school

LXVI.

To do the will of Him above.
　　Now lead me to thy daughter fair;

For her all deathless is my love.
  Ah! holy angels! what is there?"
Beside the prostrate form he fell;
  The icy hands he madly clasped,
A groan of death-like anguish welled
  Up from his faithful heart at last.

LXVII.

"My life, my love, my martyred one,
  Before me to high heaven thou'rt flown,
But soon I'll follow where thou'rt *gone*;
  Thou shalt not dwell above alone."
With hand as swift as lightning flash
  He drew his tried and trusty blade;
One glance of hatred round he cast,
  Then low before them he was laid.

LXVIII.

The life-blood from his faithful breast
  Mingled with that of Astreanere,
Whose marble hands he fondly pressed;
  He died without a sigh of fear.
And thus perished the fated two,
  Who loved while life to them was given;
Their hearts through joy and woe were true,
  And pure as stars that gem the heaven.

LXIX.

When thwart the dusky brow of night,
  The queen of space doth slowly sail,
Wearing her crown of beauty bright,
  While diamonds gem the purple vail

3

That shrouds her form, peerlessly fair,
　From mortal eyes, that as her peer,
As proudly pure, as strangely rare,
　Were Glenwold and sweet Astreanere.

LXX.

Years, years have fled and still the tale
　By Cornish peasants oft is told,
Who point with visage awed and pale,
　To a lone graveyard, grim and old,
Wherein the knight and Astreanere
　Were by the weeping Montague laid,
To rest in peace, devoid of fear,
　Their graves were by his proud hands made.

LXXI.

Toward the sinking of the sun,
　Young Glenwold's couch of gloom was placed,
And to the rising of the moon,
　Sweet Astreanere's lone palace faced;
But e'en in death they would not part;
　Up from each mound there swiftly sprung
An ash-tree, growing from the heart,
　Erelong their branches closely clung.

LXXII.

Strange, strange, they seem with arms twined,
　Leaning across that gloomy space,
Each year they grow in strength and pride,
　And closer in that fond embrace;
While on each eve of the New Year,
　Montague's old halls doth blaze with light;
And when the midnight hour is near,
　A spectral train hovers in sight.

LXXIII.

There dames of high and noble state,
　With hawks and gallants glide along,
There with his bride, Cecil elate,
　Leads on the weird, ghostly throng.
The ruined chapel, grim and hoar,
　As in the feudal days agone,
Reviews the scene of woe once more
　In all its horror, and anon

LXXIV.

The death-moan of the hapless bride
　Greets the brave watcher's startled ear.
Then Glenwold falls the maid beside,
　And then the ghosts all disappear;
Rending the midnight with a wail
　That thrills the strongest heart with fear,
Thus ends the strangely mournful tale
　Of Glenwold and sweet Astreanere.

The Battle of Brandywine.

I.

MORN rises from the brow of night,
In mystic radiance warm and bright;
And Sol, the royal god of day,
Bemounts his car in proud array.
　　Along the eastern horizon,
Soft steals a flush of rosy morn ;
　　And kissing, is the golden sun,
The dews from leaflet, flower and thorn.

II.

Up from the valleys floats the mist,
　　Borne on the gentle zephyr's wing,
In fleecy clouds it mounts to heaven,
　　As if of life and love a thing.
And as it passes from our view,
　　Ah! what a picture we behold;
A vale that's rich in flowers and fruits,
　　Whose wealth and beauty ne'er was told.

III.

There, clad in nature's green attire,
　　The giant oaks uprise so grand,
And flashing 'neath Aurora's fire

The Brandywine flows through the land.
All, all is peace and calmness now ;
   No sound disturbs the hush of morn,
Save cooing of the turtle-dove,
   Or clarion of the hunter's horn.

IV.

Bright, bright the scene that greets the eye,
For nature, rich in poesy,
Hath lavished on this beauteous vale
Her rarest treasures, from the gale
That fain would sweep athwart its breast,
And from its bosom rudely wrest
The princely trees that gem the mead,
Like sentries placed the foe to heed,

V.

And proudly stand erect.   Their brows
But to the passing whirlwind bows,
(As soldiers e'er their chief salutes,)
But all its strength to crush refutes ;
Thus e'er with kingly heads on high,
They mu'ely point toward the sky,
To which, from floral censers, rises
The morn's sweet incense.   Swiftly flies

VI.

The lark rejoicing on her way,
Chanting her trancing, matin lay,
Pouri g to Him that reigns above,
Forth all her thrilling songs of love.
The h lls of rarest emera'd green,
E'er guards this beauteous vale serene ;

Nor cloud of woe, nor shade forlorn
E'er gloomed its breast till this fair morn.

VII.

As higher rides the glorious sun,
Like banner of rare brightness, flung
Far o'er the velvet, sloping lawns
That flash with dew gems.   Where the fawns
Aneath the young moon's silver ray,
Join zephyrs light and fairies in play.
Mark well yon somber, deep, green wood,
Where myriad forms seem robed in blood.

VIII.

Where, casting back each golden beam,
Ten thousand lances brightly gleam;
Now let your wandering glances stray
Toward the dawning of the day,
And view the hills whose wild, rich blooms
Exhale a thousand rare perfumes,
And scan the blue-robed columns long,
That round yon snowy tent now throng.

IX.

Mark well the arms these warriors bear,
Then ask amazed, "Now what is there?"
I'll answer.   'Tis the Union bands
Of Columbia's sons, and in their hands
Their tried and trusty weapons are,
Which soon will gleam 'mid shut of war;
While those deep lurking in the wood,
Bedressed in garb the hue of blood,

Are Britain's reckless, hireling hordes;
For pelf, not freedom, fla h their swords.

X.

And on this calm and beauteous morn,
Instead of clang of huntsman's horn,
Or coo of gentle turtle-dove,
Or e'en the songs of deathless love,
Breathed by nature's choristers gay,
In forest green, on mountain gray,
The hills and dells w ll echo far
The fearful din of murderous war.

XI.

O Muse, heroic Mars divine,
Minerva, queen of wars sublime,
Great Jove, dread thunderer of the world,
Proud Perseus, who erstly hurled
The Gorgon monster from its power,
And Hercules, strength is thy dower,
Impart thou with the immortal four:
Strength, eloquence, poesy, lore,

XII.

That I in numbers fiery bold,
May paint those scenes, but not in gold.
Dark scenes of death's destruction dire,
Of reeking swords, of scorching fire,
Of battle shouts, of anguished moans,
Of mad despair, of frenzied groans,
Of powerless wrath, of hope divine,
That marks the day of Brandywine.

XIII.

No cloud bedims the sky of blue,
No breath disturbs the azure hue,
Cool bosom of the limpid lake,
To which the coy deer comes to slake
Its thirst.   There, on the mossy brink,
The graceful creature stoops to drink;
When lo! from out the forest shade,
Deep rolls the thunder down the glade.

XIV.

With bound as swift as fabled fawns,
The antler light flies o'er the lawns
That 'twixt its covert intervenes;
But ere its shelter safe it gains,
A leaden ball belays it low,
And on the turf its blood doth flow,
The first corse of the battle day,
Stiff, stiff and gory there doth lay.

XV.

And high above the cannon's roar,
And warring hosts on either shore,
Soaring up to the eternal skies,
The clarion tones triumphant rise,
"Remember Paoli," hear that shout
Borne on the air in thunder note,
As onward from the heart of Penn,
Cheering his troops sweeps General **Wayne**.

XVI.

Mad Anthony is now let loose;
  Britons look well unto your arms,

Lest he should pierce your gaudy troop,
   And fill your ranks with dire alarms.
"On, bruders on," hear that deep yell,
For Britons it is their death-knell ;
Three hundred braves with each a soul,
Fierce as his own follows the Pole.

XVII.

Next, with their partisans proudly free,
Come General Greene, heroic Lee,
And Waldermear, in whose dark face,
Red burns the blood of the Indian race.
'Mour the hills of Virginia, an Indian maid
Was by a British noble betrayed;
And now to avenge the embittering wrong,
'Gainst the Saxons he battles defiant and strong.

XVIII.

But who is he whose eagle eye,
Each change and movement doth descry,
With form maj stic, royal mien,
That e'en in kings is seldom seen?
How proud he sits his iron gray,
And views the soldiers' grand array ;
With heav'ng breast and kindling eye,
He marks the foemen as they fly

XIX.

Before the charge of freemen born,
The earth with nations to adorn.
But hush ! his voice loud, startling rings :
"Followers, friends of freedom's laws,
Now battling in that freedom's cause,

Who in our midst her altars placed;
Those altars with rich garlands graced,
Consisting of the noblest minds,
Impulses' deeds, blossoms divine,
That round our hearts fondly entwine.

XX.

"Before you shines, though from afar,
Sweet Independence, glorious star,
Whose lustrous, strangely luring ray,
Doth guide you on to freedom's day.
Be brave, nor falter in this hour,
In right, not might, rests all the power."
He pauses, rings an echoing cheer,
Each heart is stranger to dark fear.

XXI.

Loud roars the thunders of grim death;
Bestrewn with corses is the heath;
The scene's obscured from watching eyes,
By sulphurous smoke that dense doth rise,
And hovers like a funereal pall
O'er friend and foe, all, all
Is wrapped in deep Plutonian gloom,
Changed into somber burial tomb

XXII.

Is that fair vale which shone at morn
In nature's brightest smiling form,
No longer dancing on its way,
Or pausing with the breeze to play,
But flowing on with sluggish pace,
While corses grim its breast deface;

Torn from its banks each clinging vine,
Slow creeps the blood-stained Brandywine.

XXIII.

Amid the tried and trusty few,
Who for Columbia proudly drew
Their blades of firm unbending steel,
And taught the motherland to feel
That earth gives birth to heroes yet;
Fought freedom's friend, young Lafayette.
His boyish face with hero fire
Blazed; his trumpet voice served to inspire

XXIV.

With courage new the fainting bands.
Brief, eloquent are his commands:
" Look, brothers, mark the fiendish hordes,
'Gainst whom this day ye've drawn your swords;
The red-coat demons ne'er can know
Aught but the promptings from below;
Fight for your country, give your lives
To shield fond mothers, babes and wives.

XXV.

" Their honor to your hearts is dear,
Then faint not while one foe is near."
Thus spake the son of happy France,
'Gainst countless foes he doth advance;
When lo! from death-bestrewing balls,
A fragment on his shoulder falls,
Bleeding, half dead, 'neath murderous fire,
Slow from the field he doth retire.

XXVI.

Now who is he on night black steed,
.With eye of fire and robes of snow,
That now are stiff and stained with gore?
Ah! who can deal such fearful blows?
'Tis Pulaski, he whose iron band
Hath battled bravely for our land;
A parting blessing now he strews
Amid the hireling Hessian crews.

XXVII.

And while with rage his dark eyes burn,
Aside his head he chanced to turn,
And as he did, a sight that froze
The blood that in his proud veins glows,
His startled vision-sight grimly greets;
The foemen now our ranks defeat.
And on the brow of an emerald hill,
Adown which courses a silver rill,

XXVIII.

In whose crystal tides so softly laves
The gleaming lilies that toy with the waves,
Where the speckled trout all freely plays;
On whose mossy banks the sparrow's lays
Are heard at the dawning day,
When Aurora's light dispels the gray,
The gloomsome mantle of dreary night,
And fills all the earth with her radiance bright.

XXIX.

Close circled by three hundred foes,
The form of Washington proud uprose
There firmly sitting his iron gray,
He keeps the furious host at bay,

Nor chief nor private will dare approach
The prize, nor will he to them e'en vouch
An answer to their stern commands,
And smiles in scorn on their waving brands.

XXX.

"Surrender, if life you now would save!"
Still Washington smiles (he fears not the grave)
Nor vouches one word to them in reply
Save by the flash of his eagle eye.
At length, so sure of their noble prize,
With a shout that echoed up to the skies,
The Britons press round him, loud their cheers,
While a golden-haired captain, so young in years,

XXXI.

That Washington's heart for the brave boy bled,
So brave that the charge on their prize he led ;
An answering shout from his foes he hears,
And Washington failing to mark his men's cheers,
Grown desperate now, at the foremost he fires,
And the golden-haired captain slowly expires.
Again his pistol sharply speaks,
Another young Briton in his life-blood reeks.

XXXII.

This was the scene that greeted the eye
Of the foreign young hero, brave Pulaski.
A moment and then his iron band
Flies thundering over the gory-stained land ;
Three hundred swords then gleam in air,
Three hundred shrieks of death's despair,
And Washington again is free,
Clasping the hands of PULASKI.

Lelah Grayson.

I.

'NEATH the beeches' somber shadows,
  Through whose branches softly gleamed
Luna's , aly, silver luster,
  On her snowy brow serene ;
Waited gentle Lelah Grayson,
  For he told her meet him here,
On the green and mossy borders
  Of the brooklet singing near.

II.

Violets' azure in her tresses
  Softly bloomed, an ! on her breast
Gleamed sweet, fragrant wafer lilies,
  For he sa d, " I love them best."
In her eyes of blue-gray softness,
  Burned a strang ly lustrous fire ;
For the tones of handsome Robert,
  Did her heart with love inspire.

III.

Gently playe 1 the perfumed zephyrs,
  With the wild wood blossoms rare ;
And the night-bird sweetly warbled

Serenades to his loved one fair.
Fled the moments; lovely Lelah
  Trembled, and her lips of red
Quivered like a cherub's grieving;
  Then she heard a manly tread

IV.

Echoing down the rustic pathway.
  Then in richest music's tone,
Came the words: " My lovely Lelah,
  Have I kept you waiting lone?"
Round her waist his strong arm circled,
  To her lips he pressed his own;
In her ear his vows he breathed,
  Neath the beeches' somber gloom:

V.

" Oh, my love, my peerless darling,
  Dearer far than life to me;
Is the heart which you have given
  To my keep ng full and free?
But, sweet one, this pleasant meeting
  For long months must be our last;
On to-morrow from my old home,
  To a new one I must pass.

VI.

" Out upon the rolling prairie,
  Fortune seeking then I go;
Oh, my Lelah! oh, my Lelah!
  Will you, can you love me so?
That for months, e'en years, you'll wait me
  In your far-off northern home;

Never losing faith, but love me,
    Till to claim you I shall come?"

VII.

Then with soft eyes, tear bejeweled,
    Fondly lifted to his own,
Lelah Grayson bravely murmured:
    "I will love and wait, nor moan,
Though for years you should a-linger
    On the blooming prairies wild;
I will trust you, and, my Savior,
    True confiding as a child.

VIII.

"You will love and bravely labor,
    Waiting for the hour to come,
When with joy, and hope illuming
    Your fond heart, you'll bring me home;
And our loving Heavenly Father
    Will e'er guard us with an eye
That through ages ne'er doth slumber;
    You will claim me by and by."

IX.

"Bless you, Lelah! bless you, Lelah!
    For those words of love and cheer;
Yes, my darling, I shall claim you,
    Only trust and wait me here."
Once again her lips he presses,
    Wildly strains her to his breast:
Then a lily from her bosom
    Next his throbing heart doth rest.

X.

Softly .through the somber beeches
 Crept the young moon's silver beam,
Changing into starry jewels,
 Tears that on her lashes gleam ;
Knelt she on the dewy grasses,
 Breathing forth a fervent prayer ;
For her lover softly passes
 Gentle zephyrs through her hair.

XI.

Then arising, smiling happy,
 Faith was hers, and without lack ;
Said she: "Oh! I ne'er shall sorrow,
 For my Robert will come back."
Days swift fled till months had vanished,
 Months rolled on till years had flown ;
Till seven times the changing seasons
 Bloomed and faded. Still alone,

XII.

Lelah Grayson ever hopeful,
 Watching, waiting for her love,
Dwelt, nor dreamt of e'er distrusting
 Him whose life, all else, above,
She had prayed might be unto her
 Spared, that in the future bright,
She might of his prairie cabin ·
 Be the center shining light.

XIII.

But for years no words had reached her

4

From the wild, wild border track,
Where her lover was sojourning;
  Still, "My Robert will come back,"
Said pure faith to love a-pining,
  For the presence of its own,
For its fondly-worshiped idol:
  "Patience, soon he will be home."

XIV.

Lelah Grayson grew in beauty
  As the years swift glided on;
Many rich and noble suitors
  Loved her, urged her to don
Their proud names, but she declined them;
  Kept she in the old, old track,
Trusting, loving, hoping, saying:
  "My brave Robert will come back."

XV.

But none dreamt why she waited;
  Friends low gossiped, parents chid,
Lovers scowled, they blamed and hated,
  Knowing not that secret hid;
Nestling in her faithful bosom
  Smiled a noble-pictured face;
The bright face of handsome Robert,
  Truth and love each feature graced.

XVI.

And when lonely, sad and yearning,
  For his presence Lelah mourned;
Oft to learn faith's holy patience,
  To the flowers and sun she turned;

And she marked the eve's soft gloaming,
　And the slumbering blossoms low,
And she marked them sadly weeping
　When the sunbeams ceased to glow.

XVII.

And she saw them gladly smiling
　When the day god 'lumed earth's track;
"As the sun comes to the flowers,
　So my Robert will come back."
Then anon her heart grew lighter,
　And fair Lelah blithely sung,
And in her slightest accent
　Something wondrous gladsome rung.

XVIII.

Thus it happened on an evening
　In the month of rosy May,
To the beeches softly gloaming,
　O'er the brooklets silver way,
Gentle Lelah wandered dreaming
　Of her loved one afar;
Her sweet face of witching beauty
　Glowing brightly as a star.

XIX.

From the velvet turf she gathered
　Violets blue as heaven's skies;
From the cooling limpid waters,
　Gleaming lilies gently rise.
In her glittering, golden tresses
　Twines she nature's sapphires bright;
On her gently heaving bosom
　Placed she lilies snowy white;

XX.

Saying softly: "Robert loved them;
  Violets are like angels' eyes,
And the lilies spirits sainted
  Wear above in Paradise.
From my breast he took a lily,
  More must blossom sweetly there,
(When he comes to proudly claim me),
  And amid my golden hair.

XXI.

"Nor longer can he linger
  On the far-off prairie track;
Yes, I cull them, daily wear there,
  Soon my Robert will come back"
Rang a step adown the pathway
  Leading to the trysting brook,
Then a bronzed and stalwart stranger
  Stood within the shaded nook.

XXII.

Strange he may have been to others,
  Not quite strange to Lelah fair;
Thrice before this had she met him
  Silent, mingling, quiet, where
She as chosen belle and beauty
  Of her village queen-like reigned.
Startled was the maiden truly,
  And her terror was unfeigned.

XXIII.

"Pardon," said the handsome stranger,
  "Let me speak to you to-night;

Lelah, sweetest one, I love you,
  Pause, nor start in angry flight;
Oh long, long have I worshiped,
  Worshiped vainly from afar,
You, my rare, my peerless jewel,
  As one loves a radiant star

XXIV.

"Shining far above his station.
  Lelah, maiden sweet and mild,
Say you love me, say you love me,
  Or my poor brain will go wild."
Thrilled his accents strangely through her;
  Trembled she, not knowing why;
To refuse him made her heart bleed,
  And her soul too sadly cry.

XXV.

"Sir," said Lelah, very softly,
  With her tearful eyes a-glow;
" Smooth and even as yon brooklet's,
  Does my heart's love current flow;
Years agone my hand was plighted,
  And my heart I with it gave,
Then my lover from me wandered,
  (Frown not; pure as yon bright wave

XXVI.

Is his love and peerless honor)
  To the prairies' blooming track.
Smile not pityingly upon me;
  Soon my Robert will come back."
"LELAH!" with a cry she started,

That voice oft she'd heard before;
Smiled the bronzed and stalwart stranger.
Then, shedding her bright ray o'er

XXVII.

The pair a-neath the beeches,
 Through the heavens Luna sailed,
And the bearded face to Lelah,
 By her light was now revealed;
Oped his arms, swift to his bosom
 Flew the lovely, trembling one;
As to the ark of Noah
 Flew his bright dove, absent long.

XXVIII.

As to its mate the night-bird,
 Startled, trembling flies;
Fainting half with joy, with terror,
 Lelah in his arms lies;
O'er the wastes of barren deserts,
 O'er the prairies' blooming track,
To reclaim his bride a-waiting,
 Handsome Robert then came back.

THE
Fall of Darius Codomannus II.

I.

"ALEXANDER!" Deathless glory
  Marks the mighty conqueror's name;
Lauded in wild song and story,
  Is the ruthless monarch's fame.
Royal born, from kings descended,
  Macedonia's peerless lord;
Who on naught but hope depended,
  And his ready, trusty sword.

II.

Dark his soul as midnight ebon,
  When dense clouds doth vail the sky,
Hiding Luna's luster given,
  From the weary traveler's eye;
For his heart was full of cunning,
  Serpent-like his subtle guile;
He could fawn on those he hated,
  Mask his hatred in his smile.

III.

'Neath that wile his father suffered;
  Clitus 'neath it low expired,

(55)

Murdered by famed Alexander,
  When with wine his blood was fired;
For the monarch young and brave,
  Gave to all who dared oppose him,
Cruel death and gloomsome grave.

IV.

O'er the plains of vast Gedrosia
  Passed the monarch, breathing there,
During days of toilsome marching,
  Simoon's deadly burning air.
O'er the Indus crossed Macedon's
  Dauntless leader, crushing all,
Every nation that defied him
  Fought and bled to helpless fall.

V.

Afghan's ruler bowed submissive
  To the conqueror's galling yoke;
Egypt yielded fore the tyrant,
  Stooped his mercy to invoke;
The proud Chaldeans, crushed and humbled,
  Writhing bore Macedon's sway;
But his crowning triumph graced him
  On the field of famed Syria.

VI.

'Twas against the haughty Persian,
  Darius, that Macedon moved;
To subdue the Orient ruler,
  Macedon's chief it now behooved;
But how was the youthful monarch
  To o'ercome the Persian hosts?

Darius numbered countless soldiers,
　　Formidable the foeman boasts

VII.

Of his wealth, his mighty treasures;
　　Confident of victory, he
Marches 'gainst young Alexander,
　　One vast, moving, human sea;
Darius proudly faced the foemen,
　　Fearing not the invader's sword,
Scorning Magi's mystic warning,
　　Heedless of the prophet's word

VIII.

With his pomp his glory circled
　　Round him, Darius sought the field,
Trusting in the strength of riches,
　　Vowing that he ne'er would yield;
While to him the gods accorded
　　Life, he'd use his tempered sword,
Fighting for his honor, glory,—
　　Well the monarch kept his word.

IX.

To the battle Darius hastened;
　　Fore his army reverent borne,
Were bright silver altars chastened,
　　Whereon the eternal fires burned;
These were followed by the Magi,
　　Singing hymns along the way,
Offering praise to the all-glorious,
　　Radiant god of beauteous day.

X.

O'er three hundred youths in scarlet
  Robes, betrimmed with cloth of gold,
Served the Magi at the altars,
  Sacred scrolls of state to hold;
Then came chariots rare and costly,
  Bearing all the Orient gods,
Drawn by steeds white as the moonbeams,
  All the equerries bearing rods

XI.

Of rare gold, inwrought with jewels;
  While the great " horse of the sun "
Followed, leading the "Immortals,"
  Who full many a gift had won
From their monarch.   Golden collars
  Bound their throats and tissue robes,
Garnished o'er with gems-barbaric,
  Decked the chosen and beloved.

XII.

After came the ruler's cousins,
  Then upon a golden car,
Rode the lord of Iran's people,
  Crowned with richly-gemmed tiara;
Robed in purple, striped with silver,
  O'er his shoulders fell a mantle,
Wrought on the which with precious stones,
  Flashed the pictures of two falcons;
Battling one for prey, one for its own.

XIII.

Then came all the royal children,

With their servants, tutors grave,
Followed by the monarch's mother
 And his consort.   Truly brave
Looked the guards that them attended ;
 And robed like so many queens,
Came the beauteous royal ladies
 Of his harem ; bright, serene

XIV.

Were the jewels of his household ;
 Jealousy was then unknown
To the prides of Iran's harem,
 To love Darius all had grown.
Then came horses, patient camels,
 Bearing Persia's treasures vast,
Guarded by the light-horse lancers,
 Nowise least, though coming last.

XV.

Thus surrounded by his subjects,
 Darius marched against the foe ;
On the field of famed Assyria,
 Dealt the fiercest, wildest blow.
'Gainst the Macedon invader
 Alexander battled well ;
His proud standard rose in triumph,
 That of Darius lowly fell.

XVI.

Scattered, frightene l fled the Persians,
 Hopeless Darius followed suit ;
Vain he strove his men to rally,
 Vanquished was he then in sooth :

Macedon pursued the monarch
   Ruthless, till the Persian horde
Yielded to the grim invader,
   Putting to the reeking sword.

XVII.

Darius, their once mighty ruler,
   Crushed, deserted by his own,
In a cart, not golden chariot,
   Drew his last, deep, dying moan.
There a chief of Macedonia
  Found the expiring Darius; low
Were the words the monarch uttered,
   Said he: "Tell my generous foe,

XVIII.

"Darius prayed the gods to bless him
   For his kindness to the queen;
Chosen of the Persian monarch,
   Tell him that he honors e'en
The invader of his country;
   'Tis his prayer the universe,
Macedon may rule in future,
   Give my message to him terse.

XIX.

"Farewell, brave Macedon, farewell,
   Tell him 'tis the lot of kings
To be o'erthrown; tell him remember
   Of Darius the sufferings.
Bid him avenge my death, Macedon;
   Tell your monarch Persia's horde
But obeys its sire's mandate
   When enforced by lance and sword."

XX.

Alexander o'er the monarch
  Wept profusely, who can say
Whether 'twas from grief or pleasure
  That his foe had passed away.
He had hunted Darius ruthless,
  Hunted him to cruel death;
Then bewailed his bitter sufferings,
  When had fled that sufferer's breath.

XXI.

Thus died Darius. All his glory,
  Wealth and pomp failed to maintain
Him through the battle. Fate frowned on him;
  Death all pitiless came to claim
Him as victim for the slaughter;
  The wretched monarch low expired,
From the throne held by his fathers,
  To the tomb the king retired.

XXII.

Then his rival Alexander,
  Donned the Persian diadem,
Made himself fair Iran's ruler.
  Haughty noblemen
Scowled, complained; but Macedon
  Held the reins with iron will,
Proud defying earth's great monarch
  To subdue him. Victory still

XXIII.

Crowned his campaigns, nations trembled,
  Blood fell fast as heaven's bright rain,

Alexander's fame and glory
    Shook with terror land and main;
All the East was subdued by him,
    Save fair, famous Araby,
Where, in all its wondrous beauty,
    Springs the sweet frankincense tree.

XXIV.

'Gainst the shrine of mighty Allah
    Alexander savage turned;
To destroy the land of flowers,
    Macedonia's monarch burned;
But the God of Christian nations,
    God of earth, blue sky and sea,
Raised His hand, breathed the sentence
    That set struggling kingdoms free.

XXV.

Thus the star that rose in splendor,
    Set no more to glorious shine;
Death was lord of Alexander,
    Ended Philip's noble line.

The Haunted Well.

I.

"KATIE, pretty one, I love you,
  Will you be my little bride?'
Said young Harry, gently drawing
  The fair maiden to his side.
"Will you give yourself unto me,
  To love, cherish and protect?"
"No," cried Kate, "some other maiden,
  For your bride you must elect."

II.

Very saucy, very witching
  Looked the little beauty then;
Just such sprites are made to torture
  Tender-hearted, love-sick men.
Harry stared in wide-eyed wonder
  At the radiant fairy bright,
Surely Katie couldn't mean it
  Thus his happiness to blight.

III.

He had been so sure she loved him;
  And here, lovers, let me say
To you in secret whispers,

'Tis the swiftest, surest way
You can choose to vex a woman,
   If you love her, tell her so,
But never hint, you're sure to win her,
   This, in confidence, you know.

IV.

Like a queenly little coquette,
   Katie tossed her pretty head;
Then alas! for perverse woman,
   From his side she swiftly fled;
For the willful tears, so traitorous,
   Were flooding her bright eyes;
Now she sought to keep them secret,
   Katie was so very wise.

V.

On she flew like young fawn startled,
   Till she reached an arbor where
Sweet wild-roses, honeysuckles
   Blended scent and blossoms rare;
And a crystal fountain flashing
   In the sun's resplendent ray,
Gemm d the flowers and the vine leaf,
   With its cooling silver spray.

VI.

Here she paused, sad, half repenting
   Of her willful conduct, vain
Had she been, but sure her lover
   Would be with her soon again.
"If he does not come I'll hate him,
   If he does——" she laughed outright

As she viewed the sad face pictured
By her memory fresh and bright.

VII.

"He was so very sure I loved him,
Vain, conceited, I must say;
No, he is the dearest fellow,
Oh why did I run away?
He is coming, yes, I'll linger,
Here for a little while,
Selfish was he thus to wile
Me scowling on my other suitors.

VIII.

"Why, there's handsome Charlie Grey,
I'll accept him, no I hate him,
Why does Harry stay away?
I don't care, I never loved him,
Nor do I like his style,
Dark and jealous as Othello,
I'll wait another while.
And then he is so stately,

IX.

With his solemn, owl-like ways;
Harry, oh why do you linger?
Come, I'll love you all my days."
Vain were her willful pleadings,
Handsome Harry failed to come;
Angry, jealous, loving, penitent,
Poor Katie wandered home.

X.

At her lattice, late and early,
   Kept she watching down the lane;
But to her rejected Harry
   Failed to fondly come again;
So the summer with her beauties
   And her pleasures drifted on,
Till the fruitful, golden Autumn,
   Did her robes of purple don.

XI.

Still poor Katie lonely lingered,
   Watching, waiting, all in vain,
Daily grew her blue eyes sadder,
   And more bitter her heart's pain;
Darker grew the skies above her,
   And no longer hope elate
Bade her wait her recreant lover
   At the rustic cottage gate.

XII.

Thus the days passed by so weary,
   And no lover sought poor Kate;
Then unto a Gipsy seeress,
   Went the maid to learn his fate.
Said the seeress: "Of young Harry's
   Fate to thee naught can I tell,
But on the eve of All Hallows,
   Visit thou the haunted well.

XIII.

"There beyond the oak that's riven,
   By the stars' uncertain light,

Standing 'neath the vaulted heaven,
  Thou'lt behold thy mate for life."
On the eve of All Hallows,
  Katie wandered forth alone,
Thinking sadly of her lover,
  Till she reached the dark well stone.

XIV.

Then she looked, half hoping, fearing,
  There in the uncertain light
Stood her lover, handsome Harry;
  Turned she round in startled flight,
But a voice deep, rich and tender,
  Called, " My Katie, do not go;"
Then a pair of arms embraced her,
  And the captive, sobbing low,

XV.

Told him of her sweet repentance;
  Pleaded him to now forgive,
Vowing she would love him ever,
  For him would joyously live.
Then she told him of the sceress,
  Of her magic powers rare;
" Strange that she should know you, Harry,
  Is it not?"   " Yes, Katie fair.

XVI.

"For my love I too despairing,
  Sought the beldame in her cot,
Not to learn by magic power
  What would be my future lot;
But to weave some subtle trial,

Both your love and hate to test;
Then she many a plan unraveled,
  Katie, shall I tell the best?

XVII.

" Well, love, we were deep discussing,
  When we saw you coming fair ;
Now recall the curtained recess,
  Near the Gipsy I stood there,
And I heard your tearful query."
  Flashed her blue eyes, " Sir, how dare I
Oh I'll hate you." "No, my angel,
  For your Harry then the snare,

XVIII.

"(Cunning was it?) she set for you,
  And I caught my pretty bird ;
Don't be angry, for I love you,
  Yo`, I know we're both absurd ;
Bu` I also know, my lady,
  That your heart was breaking slow."
Held he fast the angry beauty,
  Lest she from him 'gain would go.

XIX

But at length she grew submissive,
  Tender, joyous as a dove,
And she laughed with handsome Harry
  At the story of their love.
Years have fled since that reunion,
  Happy, blest and gay they dwell ;
And on each eve of All Hallows,
  Tell they of the haunted well.

An Evening Dream.

I.

'TWAS eve, that calmly witching hour
When beauty shines with all her power;
The stars were gemming the azure sky
The moon shone in her brilliancy;
The earth in robes of green was clad,
The flowers were slumbering in their bed;
The wind sighed softly 'mong the trees,
It was the hour of rest and ease.
The night-bird warbled forth his song,
The cricket chirped loud and long;
The balmy air was with fragrance fraught,
It was the hour of love and thought.

II.

I sat me by a silvery stream
That rippled 'neath bright Luna's beam;
I sat me there to dream a while
Of flowery land and sea-girt isle;
Oh they were bright and strangely grand,
The thoughts that wandered through my mind,
Until the touch of a fairy hand,
Aroused me from my beauteous dreams.
It was a wondrous, glorious scene

(69)

That met my wildered wakening ;
For round me strewn on every hand
Lay wealth from thousand different lands.

III.

The gold ore so rich and pure,
Lay on the murmuring streamlet's shore,
And on a throne with royal mien,
There I beheld of wealth the queen;
And with a smile, pleasing to see,
The regal lady turned to me.
"O child of earth, accept," said she,
"The gift that I'll bestow on thee;
But bow thy head before my shrine,
And nameless wealth shall then be thine."
"O Wealth," I cried, " thy bounty's great,
But of it I may not partake ;
To bow my head before thy shrine,
Thy gift must be far more divine.":

IV.

My temptress vanished and instead,
Fair Venus raised her rose-crowned head ;
Her chariot was an ivory shell
Drawn by the fleetest, whitest swans;
Her purple mantle wrought with gems,
Was loosely o'er her shoulders flung.
Three graces bright around her stood,
Two Cupids at her sides with floods
Of love were seen ; holding her train
The handsome youth, Adonis, came.

V.

I gazed in wonder and surprise   .

Upon the queen of rare beauties,
As with her most bewitching smile
She offered me her gift sublime.
"A maid of beauty thou shalt be,
If thou wilt only worship me."
" O Venus fair, thy gift is rare,
But thy beauty I can not share ;
To none but Him who reigns above,
Can I my adoration prove."

VI.

The goddess left my wondering sight,
And Jupiter came in his might,
Holding the thunders in one hand,
The other held his cypress wand ;
Extending forth his strong right hand,
The one that held the flaming brand,
Said : " Maid of earth, thy courage school,
And learn the Thunderer's dread to rule;
But kneel thou at my royal throne,
And all this power will be thine own.
"Ah ! Jove," I said, " Great power is sweet,
But great and dread is thy deceit ;
For should I yield unto thy power,
Like Metis, thou mightst me devour."

VII.

Aghast the Thunderer mutely stood,
With rage untold boiled fierce his blood;
Then he raised his fiery, hissing brands
To crush me to the gleaming sands,
But Peace her olive wand between
Us thrust, me from his wrath to screen.

VIII.

The Thunderer melted like a cloud,
And I beheld the god of love;
His robes were from the roses spun,
With broken hearts his spear was strung;
And wrought in most exquisite art,
He poised his fatal, jeweled dart.
In tones of witching music low,
Said he: " Ill pierce thy young heart through,
Thou, who with beauty unadorned,
The Thunderer of Olympus scorned;
I'll melt thy heart of frigid ice,
I'll crush it in love's cruel vice."
" Ha ! ha ! avaunt, thou little wretch,
My heart is steel unto thy touch ;
On earth to thee it ne'er shall bow,
Go, little mischief-maker, now."
He turned him round, and well I know,
Though blind, he saw which way to go.

IX.

The god scarce left me when there came
In robes of snow, the queen of Fame ;
In one fair hand she held the wreath,
The wreath that thousands vainly seek,
In voice of silv'ry clearness low,
She bid me 'fore her then to bow.
" The gift of wealth thou hast declined,
Of beauty thou hast cast aside,
Of power and love thou hast disdained,
Now thou art Honor's gifted child;
Then lowly bend this head of thine,

In Fame's immortal circlet shine,
Walk in the narrow path to God;
Guided by pure Virtue's rod,
And Love and Wealth and Power will grace
Thy life one long, long hour of peace.
I raised my eyes to thank the queen,
I woke TO FIND IT ALL A DREAM.

Love and Ambition.

I.

Seated were two lovely sisters,
  In a tiring chamber, where
Maids from sunny France's bosom,
  Decked each peerless maiden.   Rare
Jewels on their bosoms sparkled,
  And upon their robes of snow,
Bridal flowers, rare and fragrant,
  Too were seen to sweetly blow.

II.

Claudia, eldest of the sisters,
  Darkly beautiful and proud,
Was regal as a youthful empress;
  . From her haughty head a cloud
Of rich, silken curls, purple
  As the raven's polished wing,
Swept a-down her sloping shoulders;
  And in every perfumed ring

III.

Flashed a gem of wondrous beauty;
  And upon her queen-like brow,
Bloomed a crown of orange blossoms,
  (74)

Purely br'ght as v rgin snow.
In her eyes of dusky splendor,
　Hovered pride and joy and mirth;
But to love's all-tender luster,
　Those rare orbs failed to give birth.

IV.

But aneath this mask of glory,
　Lurked a grievous, heartsick pain;
For proud Claudia crushed her sole love,
　Wealth, unbounded wealth to gain.
Near her sat her lovely sister,
　Radiant, happy as a dove;
'Mid her glittering golden tresses,
　Nestled gifts of her true love.

V.

Lilies gathered from the valley,
　And upon her heaving breast
Sparkled sapphires rich and lustrous,
　As the gems on royal crest;
Love-light in her eyes of azure,
　Danced like fairies when at play
'Mong the violets and the moonbeams,
　Full of mirth and mischief gay.

VI.

" Lulu," spoke the peerless Claudia,
　" Tell me why you choose to wed
With a poor and struggling artist,
　Scarce can he afford you bread?
Foolish are you, little sister,
　With a fortune in your grasp,

To forego it for a passion
   That through want can never last.

VII.

"Well I know, my darling Lulu,
   That most tenderly you love;
But to win wealth is the motto
   Which we should, all else above,
Cling to firm, ever unbending.
   Wealth and love for you and me
To receive, is such a blessing,
   That our fates will not decree.

VIII.

"I have loved, my little sister,
   And I thought that love was dead,
But to-night it wakes to haunt me
   Like a mocking spirit dread.
'Yond the heaving Spanish ocean,
   Don Alonza now doth roam;
But my heart rebellious, Lulu,'
   For his love to-night doth moan.

IX.

"Yes, I love him, little sister,
   Though this is my wedding night;
Tremble not, my angel Lulu,
   What I say is far from right;
And yet if Don Alonza
   Came to sue my hand again,
His strong love would be rejected,
   Though the torture turned my brain."

X.

"Claudia," faltered gentle Lulu,
  Gazing in her dusky face;
"Why, oh why, will you thus suffer,
  When a word would bring you peace?
He to whom you are plighted,
  Deems that his is all your love;
Sister, if your soul you'll perjure,
  A fell curse 'twill surely prove."

X1.

"Hush, your words may prove prophetic,"
  Cried proud Claudia, paling now;
Hark the summons to the bridal,
  Smooth those wrinkles from your brow."
Down the broad and gilded stairway,
  Swept the white-robed bridal train;
While within the lighted parlors
  Stood the eager guests all fain,

XII

Would behold the peerless sisters,
  Who outshone all others far;
Each a flower of brightest beauty,
  Each a radiant, glowing star.
Soon the magic words were spoken,
  Soon each maiden was a bride;
One to deathless joy was bounden,
  One to life-long woe was tied.

XIII.

Claudia to a brown-stone palace
  Went to live, resplendent shone

This proud beauty in the setting
    Wealth, that in her heart had sown
Such dark seeds of darker sorrow;
    Thorns of lost love rankled there,
And the face of young Alonza,
    Haggard, haunted her where'er

XIV.

She might seek to shun its presence;
    In the crowded ball-room gay,
'M 1 her friends at festive banquet,
    Still it mocked her night and day.
Lulu to a Western city,
    With her Willie chose to rove;
Poor in gold, but rich prodigal,
    Rich in beauty, youth and love.

XV.

Winter fled and gay spring blossomed,
    Springtime faded, summer shone,
In her robes of green and crimson,
    Autumn reigned when she had flown;
Autumn dressed in gold and purple,
    Russet-brown and glowing red,
Winter grimly then succeeded
    With his snow-crowned, hoary head.

XVI.

Thus the seasons bloomed and faded,
    Till ten years had vanished quite;
And it happened in midwinter
    On a dark and chilly night,
A close carriage, slowly driven,

Wound along a lonely street,
Pausing 'fore a stately mansion
From which floated strangely, sweet

XVI

Strains of rare and witching music;
   And upon the snowy pave
Poured a flood of mellow gaslight,
   As of gold a liquid wave.
Sounds of mirth, the songs of childhood,
   Pattering swift of tiny feet,
Musical and cheery laughter
   The passer-by doth gayly greet.

XVIII.

From the carriage stepped a lady,
   Shrouded in the deepest black;
Droopingly she slow approached
   The great house, not looking back;
Soon the bell's clear, silver summons
   Opened wide the hall-way door,
Then the weary, black-robed stranger
   Sank upon the marble floor.

XIX.

To her side a lovely lady,
   Golden-haired, with eyes of blue,
Trembling with tender compassion,
   Quickly sympathetic flew.
Then the vail of crape was lifted
   From the cold, cold pallid face;
"Claudia! sister!" cried fair Lulu,
   "For you now this is no place."

XX.

Soon within a luxurious chamber,
  On a snowy, downy bed
Claudia lay, from her forever
  Was her royal beauty fled.
Soon the sad and mournful story
  By the hapless one was told,
And the bitter lesson learned
  By all who sell themselves for gold.

XXI.

"Lulu," said the dying Claudia,
  "For awhile I fondly dreamed
That great wealth would heal the love-wound
  In my heart, for so it seemed;
For a time I thought me happy,
  Happy in my Harry's love,
And I strove to teach my poor heart
  To return his noble love.

XXII.

"But alas! for outward seeming,
  Soon I wearied of the bond
Wrought of gold, that firmly bound me
  To a man o'er proud and fond;
Restlessly with him I wandered
  From foreign land to land,
Vainly praying for my lost peace;
  Ever on my wan left hand

XXIII.

"Shone the ring which said you're wedded,
  Tauntingly, ruthless and dread,

Till I cried out in my anguish:
    Oh I wish my heart was dead.
In a pretty little hamlet,
    When Queen Summer reigned supreme,
Sought I with my tender husband,
    Safe retreat in sunny Spain.

XXIV.

"On a lovely, starlight even,
    As idly through an orange grove,
I lone wandered, there, ah Heaven!
    I beheld my banished love ;
Darkly, wild and full of sorrow
    Looked Alonza once so fair,
Silver threads were softly gleaming
    In the midnight of his hair.

XXV.

" With a glad, glad cry of rapture,
    Don Alonza reached my side,
Clasped me to his wild bosom,
    Dreaming not I was a bride.
'Claudia! oh my peerless Claudia !'
    Cried he, 'My heart's bright dove,
Have you come to make me happy
    With your rare and royal love?

XXVI.

"'Long I've watched for you, my jewel,
    Long I've watched you from afar,
Waiting patient for your coming,
    As the wise men watched the star

6

Of Bethlehem in the desert;
   Now my royal rose you're here,
Fate itself can never part us,
   Promised bride of mine most dear.'

XXVII.

"'*Traitoress!*' Never, Lulu, gentle sister,
   Never more can I forget
That one word, as sad reproachful
   As the bitter sigh of death.
From Alonza's arms I tore me,
   There my noble husband stood,
Me regarding with such glances
   As almost froze my blood.

XXVIII.

"Soon he spoke in icy accents:
   'Well I know what sorrow now
Ever in your proud heart rankled,
   That e'er gloomed your lovely brow,
'Twas your love for this young brigand;
   Traitoress! soon he'll meet his fate,
Come though false as mocking mirage,
   Still you are my wife.' Too late

XXIX.

"Came the startled cry I uttered;
   Swift as lightning's lurid ray,
Flashed aloft Alonza's dagger,
   Dead before me Harry lay.
Years have fled, Alonza loved me
   In his wild, untutored way;
Closely guarded in a lone cave,
   Dwelt I wretched night and day,

XXX.

"Till the countless Spanish legions
  Scattered wide the outlaw band,
Till I saw my second husband lying low
  With his own hand.
When o'ercome by cruel foemen,
  He had closed his gloomy life,
Calling on me soon to follow;
  Murmuring: 'Bless my lovely wife.'"

XXXI.

Claudia paused, her tears were falling;
  Lulu smiled, half hopeful now,
As with tender, loving pressure,
  She gently bathed her burning brow.
Soon poor Claudia resumed saying:
  "From Alonza's mountain cave
I was taken weak and weary,
  The dark outlaw's captive slave.

XXXII.

"None e'er dreamt of how I loved him;
  Pity was the balm they gave,
And they bade me thank my Maker,
  That from death I had been saved;
Then I begged that I might hasten
  To the free land of my birth;
And the kindly Spaniards sent me
  To destroy your peace and mirth.

XXXIII.

"Lulu when our paths were chosen
  I was very poor and proud;
I crushed love and married riches,

Love you chose, nor feared want's cloud;
  You are happy, I am wretched,
    Two hearts in the dust I trod,
Both lie cold and pulseless, Lulu,
    'Neath the dark and gloomy sod.

XXXIV.

"I have naught to live for, sister,
    Save the stings of conscious dread;
Farewell, Lulu, don't forget me,"
    And the hapless one lay dead.
From Claudia's brow the sister
    Wiped the chilling dews of death,
While her tears of love and sorrow
    Mingled with her latest breath.

XXXV.

Knelt fair Lulu at the bedside,
    Breathing forth a fervent prayer:
"I, my Heavenly Father, thank thee
    For thy gifts and blessings rare;
For my husband's love all deathless,
    For my babes of beauty bright;
And I thank thee, Heavenly Father,
    For sure guiding me aright."

XXXVI.

Lulu mourned for her sister,
    When they had laid her low,
'Neath the drooping, weeping willow;
    On her grave bright blossoms grow,
And she thanks her Heavenly Father,
    That to her he deigned to unfold
The strange mysteries blest of wedding,
    For sweet love and not for gold.

The Warrior's Fate.

I.

THROUGH the streets of famed Strasburg,
  Two noble youths passed;
Just verging on manhood,
  Yet with the boys classed.
Karl, tall, manly,
  Bold, dashing, his eye,
Blue, dauntlessly flashing,
  Seemed fear to defy.

II.

His proudly-poised head,
  With rich golden hair crowned;
His high, thoughtful brow
  With bright curling locks bound,
Told of a grand soul,
  Calm, abiding within;
Told of talent, of genius,
  That fame's laurels might win.

III.

Oh fond was the mother
  That called him her son;
(85)

Oh happy the maid
  Whom his true heart won;
Oh proud was the father
  That called him his own,
And honored the friends
  That his friendship had known.

IV.

Right merry they walked
  Through the over-thronged street,
Conversing and laughing
  In gayety sweet.
When lo! on the air
  They heard the loud call
Of the warrior's trumpet
  Startingly fall.

V.

" Hark! Henry," cried Karl,
  " What means that loud call?
Why hasten those people,
  Men, women and all?"
" Because," said his friend,
  " We're at war with the French;
They our honor and glory
  From us fain would wrench."

VI.

" 'Tis the call of our country,"
  Then Karl declared;
" Oh, Henry! 'tis even
  As grandfather feared;
Our men must take arms,

Our women must toil,
Or the foe o'er our nation
Will ravage and spoil.

VII.

"We must fight, dearest Henry,
Our country to save,
The foe shall be vanquished;
In gore we must lave
Our blades ever trusty,
And when we return
From the war, on fame's tablets
Our names bright shall burn.

VIII.

"Our mothers rejoicing,
Shall bless their brave sons,
Our silver-haired sires
Shall treasure the guns
Used by their brave boys;
And our sweethearts shall sing
From excess of their joy,
Loud their anthems shall ring."

IX.

Oh little dreamt Karl,
As gayly he spoke
These words, half prophetic,
That death's fatal stroke
Would bow his proud head,
Crowned with golden hair bright;
From the soulful blue eyes,
Strike the bold hero light.

X.

His friend sa ly sighed
  As he gazed on the boy,
And he pitied his parents;
  The maiden whose joy
Was wrapped in the life
  Of the heroic youth,
And he groaned in his heart
  As he guessed at the truth.

PART SECOND.

XI.

Through the streets of famed Strasburg,
  A gallant band moved,
In whose midst handsome Karl,
  The dearly beloved,
Was seen proudly marching;
  His golden head high,
While the hero light dauntless,
  Bold flashed in his eye.

XII.

His friend, thoughtful Henry,
  Kept pace at his side;
Nor prouder, more joyous,
  E'er passed a young bride
From the home of her parents,
  Than Karl the fair;
No prince of blood royal,
  Ever boasted his air.

XIII.

Before quiting his home
  For the tent and the field,
Young Karl sought Lena,
  To whom he did yield
His boy-heart impulsive;
  With passionate fire
He told her his dreams,
  His ambitious desire

XIV.

To become a great hero.
  Poor Lena but wept,
To the breast of her lover
  All trembling she crept,
And sobbed, "Oh, my Karl,
  Why must you away?
There are thousands and thousands
  To join in the fray.

XV.

"Then forego your ambitions,
  Nor leave me alone;
What is glory to me,
  I want naught but my own."
"Hush, Lena, my angel,"
  Young Karl then said;
" Oh surely, my love,
  You're a patriot maid.

XVI.

" I will be a great captain,
  Or colonel perhaps;

Then you'll love me the more
  For my bright shoulder straps."
" No, Karl, my lover,
  The glitter and glare
Of uniforms gay,
  I am ready to spare.

XVII.

" I never admired
  The trappings of war;
Its murderous weapons
  I'll ever abhor.
Frown not, dearest Karl,
  I know you are bold,
Patriotic and brave;
  But your glory and gold

XVIII.

" Now decks your proud head
  Like a crown from on high;
Oh leave me not, Karl; .
  What if you should die?"
" Then, Lena, my name
  In rich letters of gold,
On the scroll-book of fame,
  The tale would unfold;

XIX.

" Of how in the morning
  Of glorious youth,
I laid down my life
  For my country—in sooth,
Dear Lena, I've listed,

Weep not, neither mourn;
Soon covered with glory
To you I'll return."

PART THIRD.

XX.

Through the streets of famed Strasburg,
A long column brave
Moved, bearing a comrade
To the warrior's grave.
The dark bier was draped
With the flag he bore
Through the black smoke of battle,.
The doomed line before.

XXI.

When they faced the grim foemen,
The young bear r grand,
Fought well for his country
With his goodly right hand;
He defended his colors,
And when officers quailed
He cheered on the bold legion,
Though by battle smoke vailed.

XXII.

In the front of the battle
They saw his hair shine,
Like the crown of an angel,
Seeming half divine;

They follo ed t trusting,
  Confiding and bold—
That proudly-poised head
  With its halo of gold.

XXIII.

As followed the comrades
  Of Henry of France,
(Their monarch) bold pressing
  Where h.s snowy plume glanced;
So followed the Prussians
  Young Karl, the brave,
Lighted onward to triumph
  By the glory-bright waves

XXIV.

Of hair that around
  His kingly head shone.
To the heart of the hero,
  Grim fear was unknown;
Oh bravely he fought,
  By vast numbers oppressed;
He must yield his loved flag
  Or receive in his breast

XXV.

The weapons of death,
  By grim foemen swift hurled.
If lost were his colors,
  What to him was the world;
For he scorned a life,
  When bought at the price
Of his honor; *no, never!*
  Let his blood then suffice.

XXVI.

But while in his arm
  An atom of strength
Remained, his loved flag,
  Though woefully rent,
He'd defend,
  Come what may;
There he stood like a lion
  When keeping at bay
The hunters, though armed
  With merciless steel,
It fights fiercely on,
  Not seeming to feel
The pain of its wounds;
  And its last bitter groan
Is a growl of defiance,
  More than a death-moan.

XXVII.

So stood noble Karl,
  Staunch, keeping at bay
The host that pressed on him;
  Just as he gave way,
Sinking, wounded to death,
  His comrades appeared;
Too late to the rescue,
  As anguished they feared.

XXVIII.

The hero was dying,
  The battle was won;
And he smiled fondly saying:
  " Tell my father his son

Fought well his dear country's
   Bright honor to save;
Tell him, Henry, my brother,
   Not to weep o'er my grave.

XXIX.

" Oh tell my fond mother,
   That her first-born boy
Preferred death to dishonor;
   And, Henry, decoy
From her grief my poor Lena;
   To me you've been true,
Then win her love, brother,
   I give her to you.

XXX.

" But if she clings unto
   My memory then,
Be her comfort and solace,
   Friend, bravest of men;
Tell Lena that to her
   My last thoughts were given;
Farewell, dearest Henry,
   We'll all meet in heaven."

XXXI.

With mournful faces
   And muffled drum beat,
With solemn tread
   Of the martial feet,
They bore him in sorrow
   To the gloomsome tomb,

And many a hero
  Wept over his doom.

XXXII.

Oh deep was the grief
  In each warrior's breast;
With unnatural gloom
  The band was oppressed;
Though victory had crowned
  The great German host,
Their loved color-bearer,
  Forever was lost.

XXXIII.

No more would the golden
  Crowned head 'fore them shine,
No more would they follow
  Its guidance divine;
No more would the blue eyes
  With hero light flash;
· Or ne'er would he wear
  His well-won sword and sash.

XXXIV.

And Lena, his darling,
  Wept at the tomb;
Upbraiding the fates
  For his untimely doom;
Sadly heart-rending her cry
  As she wailed,
" Oh! my Karl,
  Oh! why did you die?"

XXXV.

But the cold lips were mute,
  And the azure eyes dim,
That late danced all joyous;
  Death had chosen him.
The golden locks waved
  O'er the grand, noble brow
That late bore the mpress
  Of beauty and thought,
With heroic courage
  And boyish pride fraught.

XXXVI.

So in silence and sorrow,
  They consigned to the **tomb**
The hero of Strasburg,
  In the beauty and bloom
Of manhood, down-stricken
  By the hand of grim death;
Leaving Lena to mourn
  With her last sighing breath.

XXXVII.

And daily the maiden
  Doth visit the tomb,
Bestrewing it over
  With Flora's sweet bloom;
And soon will she follow
  Where Karl has flown;
To the spirit-land beauteous,
  Where grief is unknown.

Mohammed.

I.

"MOHAMMED!" Deathless till the world
    Attains its sure, but dreaded end,
That name shall live. 'Twas he unfurled
    The Islam standard, to defend
The which from wrong, from fell insult,
    He raised a mighty, powerful horde;
And heathen nations 'braced his faith
    To 'scape his dread death-dealing sword.

II.

It was in happy Araby,
    Where rarest flowers doth endless bloom,
And freighted is the balmy air
    With the rich frankincense perfume,—
Where silv'ry lakes and rosy bowers,
    The eyes of wondering man delight;
And like an empress in her hall,
    Wearing her crown of jewels bright,
Or shrouded in a purple pall,
    So proudly steps the queen of night.

III.

For she to thankless man was given
    To light his path through darkness long;

7   (97)

By her the storm-wrapt clouds are riven,
 And round her pathway gayly throng
The stars in one resplendent train,
 Like maids of famed Sultana's court,
That round their mistress doth remain ;
 Or dancing 'fore her throne doth sport.

IV.

Slow, majestic, through the blue heaven,
 Queen Luna on her silver car
Sails, shedding forth the luster given
 By Him whose eye doth see afar,
Beyond the bounds of chaos space ;
 And hung like lamps of gold above,
Depending from the concave sky,
 Bright glow the stars of hope and love.

V.

But when the day god proud doth rise,
 Mounting his car of gold on high,
Careering through the eternal skies,
 Illuming earth's arched canopy;
Making this beauteous spot so bright,
 That Allah might from heaven descend,
Bearing with him his angel choirs,
 To fill this glorious, blessed land
With music from their golden lyres.

VI.

Oh who would ever dare to dream,
As gazed he on this fairy scene,
That once this land so beauteous rare,
Was the abode of grim despair ;

Where fathers slew their daughters young,
Or into graves them living flung;
A land that was the home
Of human vultures dark that roamed
From place to place destroying life,
Spilling their blood in useless strife;
Where brother laid his brother low,
E'er deeming him his ruthless foe,
Despoiling him of all his goods,
Steeping his soul in murdered blood.

VII.

Where chieftains proud, green lizards ate,
And often famine's pangs to sate,
The husband *slew* his trusting wife,
With her remains sustaining life;
Savage devouring flesh and blood
Of her who loved through ill and good,
And ruthless rent her stiffening corse;
He loved her less e'en than his horse.

VIII.

A land where none but Ishmaels dwelt,
A land that naught but horror felt,
A land accursed by heathen pride,
A land where darkness would abide
Despite the efforts of a world,
Till Islam's banners were unfurled.

IX.

Ye Christians, horrified behold
The worship of the Islam bold;
Ye mock the Koran's mystic law,

In every rite ye find a flaw;
Ye fain would shake Mohammed's **power**,
That like Olympian mountains tower
High o'er the heathen Arab host,
That many a Moslem soul doth boast.

X.

But blame him not, God sent the man
To change each murd'rous Arab clan
From human vultures to become
The followers of a prophet brave;
A second Moses sent to save
A people lost to God and heaven;
To teach the laws Allah had given.

XI.

In Mecca, Allah's sacred shrine,
The prophet sent by will divine,
Breathed his first, his natal breath;
Born of the humblest parents 'neath
The arching sunlit Arab skies,
In which the Magi great descried
The star that o'er his birthplace shone,
The brightest orb that e'er was known
Since that rare, lustrous, guiding light,
That 'lumed the primal Christmas night;
The star that led the good, wise men,
THE GLORIOUS STAR OF BETHLEHEM.

XII.

Long, long the Magi pondered o'er,
Long, silent praying stood before
The ATTER, QUEDAH's sacred flame,

Then gave the boy his wondrous name,
"MOHAMMED!" born to never die,
While live the waters, earth and sky;
And now the Moslem seals his word,
E'er by his tomb, long beard or sword.

XIII.

'Twas in the month through which prevailed
Unbroken peace, that he revealed
Unto the pilgrims, Gentiles, Jews,
Arabs, Chinese and staid Hindoos,
The truths the which he could instill
Into the heathen heart at will.

XIV.

Wild was the zeal by all displayed;
Bold huntsman, free, fair mountain maid,
To Islam's power low bowed their heads,
For Islam fills black hearts with dread;
The turbaned Turk and fiery Hun,
For Islam did their armor don,
And Pashas from the burning Ind
Came with horsetails streaming in the wind.

XV.

The Hindoo proud forsook the wave
Of Gunga, where so oft he laved
And took the Koran for his guide,
Nor feared the wrath of Gange's tide.

XVI.

Long, long the mighty Khaliph fought,
With grand success his reign was fraught;

Triumphant rang the glorious cry,
That echoed to the eternal sky:
"Allah, Il Allah," God is God,
Let infidels weep 'neath the rod
Of iron-edged with avenging steel,
Let heretics its horrors feel,
Let all who mock Mohammed's word
Fall 'neath his death-bestrewing sword.

XVII.

Kings, Sultans, Khaliphs, Pashas, all,
With bounding hearts answered the call
Of Islam's strangely powerful voice,
It made the hardest heart rejoice;
All yielded to Mohammed's power;
They vowed the Koran to obey,
And with the bright and ready sword,
For Islam fought till Jezdegerd,

XVIII.

The lord of lords and king of kings,
Self-styled received with proud scornings,
The messenger Mohammed sent;
Shaikh Maghurah, who intent
On changing the proud Sultan's heart,
Rejoicing hastened to impart
The tidings glad to Jezdegerd,
Who with contempt the message heard.

XIX.

Then said the monarch with disdain,
With ruthless tongue and haughty mien:
"Who is this man that durst demand

From the great lord of Persia's land
Tribute? A namcle-s upstart he,
Who soon will craving mercy be;
Cowering object at my feet,
Go tell him Jezdegerd doth greet,

XX.

As Khaliphs none but Khaliphs born,
His religion, peace, from him I scorn;
Shaikh Maghurah, false and vain
Is he that boldly doth proclaim
Himself great Allah's prophet sent
The sins of men, or e'en prevent
Them from adoring aught they will,
Sun, moon or stars or vernal hill;
Go tell your master, Jezdegerd
His messages with scorn has heard,
Tell him some gifts of wheat and wine,
He'll send the prophet now divine;
But tribute he shall never pay,
Nor bow his head to Islam's sway."

XXI.

When Omar heard this bold reply,
With fiery wrath kindled his eye;
Unfurling Islam's banners wide,
Prepared to crush the Persian's pride.
The Sultan smiled with mocking laugh,
He taunted Omar, urged him quaff
The draught of woe he held in store,
For Islam's chief he longed to soar
High up to Fame's celestial throne,
And on his forehead wear her zone.

XXII.

But vain, vain was Jezdegerd's boast,
He met brave Omar's serried host,
And humbly bowed to Islam's sway,
On the red field " Cadessia ; "
Jezdegerd fled before his foes,
Upon his soul a horror grows
That he should fall, become the prey
Of Islam's Khaliph ; day by day
He lurked in secret ambush laid ;
Few friends were his, the Moslem blade
Had awed the Persian hordes ;
No more they loved their lord of lords.

XXIII.

At length the wretched, homeless king,
That once his own praises could sing,
Unto a miller hard appealed
For shelter, food ; pledges he sealed
With gifts of rare and costly gems,
That flashed once on his diadems.
The miller granted his request,
And while he slumbered, deep the breast
Of Persia's mighty ruler pierced
His dagger keen, avaricious, fierce,
And robbed the murdered corse so cold,
Taking his robe 'broidered with gold,
The jewels of his mantle wide,
And silver sword sheath from his side.

XXIV.

Thus died the haughty Jezdegerd,
Not by the warrior's flaming sword,

But in the dead of gloomsome night,
The assassin's hand his soul set free,
And sent it to eternity;
While Omar ruled the Persian hordes,
Their king of kings and lord of lords.

XXV.

The Moslems prospered, and in time
Their strength and power seemed half divine;
Thus Christian nations looking on,
Oft wonder how such deeds are done;
While nations rise and fall,
While ministers of the Gospel call,
To the Christians them to heed,
As lessons precious loud they read
From Christ's great book of holy law,
In which the soul can find no flaw;
They careless view the beauteous ray,
That lights of heaven the narrow way;
The Koran is the Moslem's guide,
And by its maxims they abide.

The Miser Outwitted.

I.

MOSES VANHOLSTEIN was a Jew,
   And miser of the old persuasion;
One of the rare and coward few,
   That always dread burglar invasion.
Rich, rich was he in lands and gold,
   But poor as Job in human treasure;
Such as true love for kindred friends,
   Or love for heaven's eternal pleasures.

II.

Oh but he was a stingy knave,
   A skinflint granite is not harder
Than his small heart; a loaf to save
   He'd pilfer from a neighbor's larder;
But *still he was* a GENTLEMAN.
   GOLD hides a multitude of failings;
Fair damsels did our hero scan,
   And gave him countless witching hailings.

III.

Poor, proud papas oft sought him out,
   Inviting him to tea or dinner,
And rival sisters quarreled about

Him, each desirous to be winner
Of Moses' gold. Oh how he laughed
  At them, their parents, and the folly
To think he could be caught with chaff,
  And yet our friend was mighty jolly.

IV.

On those occasions, such as when
  Visiting some fair gold-sick charmer,
With appetite just three days old,
  (So said some young, gay, jesting farmer)
He would discuss the viands and wines,
  Regardless of the flesh forbidden ;
I grieve to tell the mournful truth,
  He'd eat pork pie though lost was heaven.

V.

And sausage, too, with sour krout,
  Such was his willful inclination ;
Besides the cheese, Limburger famed,
  Made in this Jew's adopted nation,
Until his host would quake with fear,
  For a skilled M. D. anxious sending;
But Moses staunch would bravely bear
  The burden, e'er triumphant ending.

VI.

Now Moses was no more a fool
  Than you or I, my gentle reader,
In fashion's van, in Mammon's school
  At Greenvale he was social leader;
Ere forty years had with their change,
  Their storms and sunshine passed o'er him,

Four gentle brides had flown away,
   And still poor Moses saw before him

VII.

Some hope of sweet connubial bliss.
   Love in his flinty heart held swaying,
And loveliness need not be his
   While such fair maids were him waylaying;
Yet he resisted all his wiles,
   Again he feared to try and marry;
"For where's the use of having wives,
   If they in life refuse to tarry?"

VIII.

At length a Christian friend who lived
   Upon the isle of famed Manhattan,
Invited Moses soon to come
   And see his daughter Flora Alton.
Miss Alton was a lovely maid,
   The skies of heaven were never bluer
Than her bright eyes; the amber shade
   Of her rich curls as gold was pure.

IX.

"The fairest maid that ever trod
   The earth," so said our Greenvale miser;
Ah! had he known what soon he learned,
   His course, I ween, it had been wiser.
The match was made, the pair were wed,
   Moses brought home his lovely treasure;
Albeit poor Flora shook her head,
   And bade farewell to future pleasure.

X.

'Twas evening of a summer's day,
  Flora Vanholstein, pale with sorrow,
Stood all alone within a room,
  (Whose very furniture would harrow
The heart of one, less used to wealth
  Than she) her eyes of azure softly shedding
Tears of unheard of undreamt woe;
  Her life's dark curse had been her wedding

XI.

With one so far beneath herself
  In moral likewise mental culture;
An angel she in woman's guise,
  He was a grasping human vulture.
The setting sun upon her shone,
  Around her dainty head a halo
Of amber ringlets bright were blown;
  Divinely fair despite the shadow

XII.

That rested on her polished brow,
  Flora Vanholstein yielded duty
Unto her cruel tyrant lord;
  Slow fading was her peerless beauty.
" Vlora, mein·frow," in accents thick
  And harsh the words were to her borne,
Then with a sigh at once heart-sick,
  Back to her life of woe she turned.

XIII.

" Now vat you vants mit grying,
  Like von schild of two year old?

Vat your tired out mit living ?
    Go dead, fast ish your fader's gold,
All your lands are in my keeping,
    All your moonish ish in bank ;
Four rich frows haf gone before you,
    Follow dem, I vill you dank.

XIV.

"Dere are oder pooty mädchens, (girls)
    Dey vould gladly marry me,
One of dem I'll choos, my lady,
    Shust so soon as I am free.
Go you now und bring my supper ;
    Hark! whose calling? Vlora dear,
Ach Got! my frow ish crazy,
    Running down the hall."   (So drear.)

XV.

Flo' Wyndham, darling sister,
    Of my love and weary heart,
Welcome to my heart though wretched,
    From you never more I'll part.
The new-comer was a lady
    Just twenty years, no more,
Tall, dusk-faced, dark-eyed, slender,
    Graceful formed as friend of yore,

XVI.

Fearless as a young knight errant,
    Chafing ever at delay ;
Young Miss Wyndham was a lady
    That would have her own sweet way.
Over Moses' Teutonic figure,

Her bright eyes derisive passed,
Then in tones, clear and ringing
  As the bugle's sweet notes, asked :

XVII.

" Friend, what are your politics ?
  For whom are you going to voto?
Is it for Grant or Greeley?
  For my part, I honor both."
For a moment Moses frowning
  Viewed the dazzling fairy bright,
Then in tones harsh as an owl's hoot
  He responded, angry light

XVIII.

Blazing in his eyes of green-gray
  Hue, just like a cat's :
" I votes dat now you leaves us,
  Mit your feathers, fuss und hats ;
You comes to see von poor mans,
  To keeps you I can't afford,
So you had better go home,
  Hasten now de train to board."

XIX.

"Keep me !" cried the taunting houri,
  " Why, you blockhead, I've a charm
By which I can live and flourish
  On the air ; don't look alarmed,
I ne'er touch the food of mortals,
  Man, I've found a magic way
That to live and thrive costs nothing
  But the will the ghost to lay."

XX.

" Vat ghost?" asked he bewildered.
  "Why the ghost of appetite ;
And now that I need not supper,
  I'll be saying you good-night."
Away they went, those lovely Floras,
  One so dark, the other fair ;
She, who fed on mortal rations,
  And the one who lived on air.

XXI.

"Are you mad?" gasped timid Flora,
  "Moses this will not believe."
" Won't he ?" laughed Miss Wyndham,
  " To me this matter leave."
Next morn' our charmed charmer
  Bright and early left her room,
Her eyes resplendent glowing,
  And her olive cheeks a-bloom.

XXII.

Moses watched her airy movements,
  And he wondered in his heart
If one so strangely lovely,
  Could exist on magic art.
Secretly he searched her chamber,
  And her trunks invaded too ;
But no hidden food unto him
  Was revealed.   Perplexed the Jew

XXIII.

Watched and waited, unrewarded
  Was his vigilance and care ;

All unconscious of his danger,
  He was falling in a snare.
So the days flew on, unheeded
  By the Floras, both intent
On some strange, mystic proceeding,
  Each the other comfort lent.

XXIV.

Suddenly Flora Vanholstein
  Laid her down, sick unto death,
Fainter daily grew her pulses,
  Fainter still her fragrant breath;
So the learned, aged physician
  Vowed his patient could not live,
And he ceased the Lodge to visit,
  And his bitter pills to give.

XXV.

Bright Flo' Wyndham ever tender,
  Cared for Moses and his wife;
Seeing that his meals were ready
  Punctual; and o'er Flora's life
Kept she faithful watch and constant,
  Death, grim monster, for to scare;—
But one night he claimed her darling,
  Claimed her friend so brightly fair.

XXVI.

Moses mourned not his treasure,
  Another bride he had in view,
And he deemed her proof 'gainst illness,
  So he from the presence drew.

8

Flo' hung o'er the lifeless Flora,
  Robed her for her final rest;
Then to gaze upon the sweet face,
  -Heartless Moses sore she pressed.

XXVII.

Said he to her long entreaty:
  "All my frows dey vants to die,
Und I dells dem shust to do so,
  Den dey mope und grieve und cry;
Ven dey weary of de pasdimes,
  Dey all goes in de bett,
Und dey pine away mit sorrow
  Till at last dey all go deat.

XXVIII.

"Vell, I goes to find anodor,
  I can nodings do but try;
Ven again I marry,
  I vill win one vat don'd cry;
So you shust nails down the coffin,
  Make it tight und fast,
I feels sick till she's buried,
  If *she vakes* my joy ish past."

XXIX.

In the eyes of fond Flo' Wyndham
  Flashed a deadly, scornful light,
And her lips of coral wreathed
  Into smiles most strangely bright,
Half of pity, half derision,
  Mingled with a flash of hate;

Moses oft recalled the vision,
　Alas for him! when 'twas too late.

XXX.

Soon the grave of lovely Flora
　Vanholstein was made, and then,
'Mid the mourning of her neighbors,
　Low the wronged young wife was lain;
Then with an aged companion,
　Flo' Wyndham slow returned
To the Lodge to find its master
　Jovial and unconcerned.

XXXI.

"Vat! my dear, now must you leaves me
　All alone, mitoud von friend?"
"No!" cried Flo', "I stay to cheer you
　Till the summer gains its end."
Moses, you may vow, was happy
　In the capture of the maid;
For never on his larder *dear*,
　Or orchard would she raid.

XXXII.

Flo' was blithe and full of mischief,
　As frolicsome magpies;
Yet she held her aged admirer
　At a distance with her eyes;
When they flashed in anger on him,
　He was humble as a slave,
And oft to hear her singing,
　Very meekly he would crave.

XXXIII.

But love is a daring fellow,
    And he made our hero bold;
So one evening, with much terror,
    To Flo' Wyndham thus he told:
"I bees rich, I've heaps of moonish,
    All vill I gif to you
If you vill mit me marry,
    And to me be efer true."

XXXIV.

"Marry you!" exclaimed the lady,
    With her black eyes flashing fire;
"Why, you blockhead, are you crazy,
    Thus to rouse my sleeping ire?
That you're rich I take for granted,
    But ere long you will be poor;
You will roam without a shelter,
    Turned from this very door.

XXXV.

"For of all the heedless spendthrifts,
    You're the greatest 'twas my chance
To see; oft I shudder
    At your mad extravagance;
I would gladly make you happy,
    But a man I'll never wed
Till he triumphs o'er his nature,
    Till he lives on air, not bread."

XXXVI.

"Oh I can nefer do dis fastings,
    It ish so very hard;

I vould surely in de trial
  To kills hunger, slowly starve."
"*Coward!* then you never loved me,
  I will leave this very night,
For I scorn the man that dare not
  CONQUER HIS OWN APPETITE."

XXXVII.

" No, pooty von, don'd leaves me,
  I vill make de trial so:
If I succeeds den you loves me,
  If I fails I die, I know."
"How are you to-day, dear Moses?"
  Soft as coo of turtle-dove,
Came the words from strange Flo' Wyndham,
  As bending anxiously above

XXXVIII.

The couch whereon the miser
  Lay, slow dying by degrees,
In his thirst for wealth and beauty,
  He renounced both *bread and cheese.*
She fixed her black eyes keenly
  On his thin and haggard face;
Well she knew that further fasting
  Would end his life's dark race.

XXXIX.

" Veaker, veaker," sighed the poor wretch,
  "I grows veaker efry day,
Vlo'. mein pooty von, dis fastings
  Don'd begin at all to pay."
"Nonsense!" cried the dazzling creature,

" You've fasted now three days,
Two more then the charm is perfect;
  With them come wealth and ease.

XL.

"But lest you should be tempted
  To indulge in former tastes,
Here are papers, deeds that make me
  Mistress of your vast estates;
You must sign them in the presence
  Of your lawyer, Mr. Hare."
"Nefer! nefer! vicked schemer;
  Oh I vonder how you dare

XLI.

" Say such tings to me? Great Fader,
  Haf I fallen in a snare?
'Tis my moonish, not my love,
  Vat you vants; I say get oud."
"Very well, my dearest Moses,"
  And the lovely creature bowed;

XLII.

" But before I leave you, Moses,
  Read those papers with calm mind;
'Tis to Mrs. Flora Vanholstein,
  That I wish the fortune signed."
"Oh! my love, come kiss me pardon,
  I vas mad mit shealous rage;
Vat a fool I bees, my sweet von,
  Vile you ish a great sage."

XLIII.

"When my name is Flo' Vanholstein,

I will give my lord salutes;
Now I must go and do the milking,
　For the market prepare fruits."
To the kitchen flew our heroine,
　And ere long a royal feast
Was in progress of preparing,
　Fit for a Sahib of the East.

XLIV.

And when the viands were ready,
　To Moses' chamber gay she hied,
And laid out the tempting dinner
　Near the famished wretch's side;
Then without a word of warning,
　Down the cruel beauty sat;
Then began to feast with relish,
　Soon, "Ach Got! now vat ish dat?

XLV.

"Surely, Vlo', you eats no such tings."
　"Yes, my friend, indeed I do,
And I never saw an idiot
　Till the day I met with you."
"But oh! my pooty darling,
　You gon not eat so much,
Gif me von little morsel or I'll die,
　I'll die in such

XLVI.

"Horrid torment; oh you can not
　Eats it all, gif me a bit."
"Yes, and more if I had it, Moses,
　Ten times more if I had it."
"*More if I had it,*" shrieked the miser,

Falling forward in a fit;
" More if I had it, if I had it,
Ten times more if I had it."

XLVII.

For a doctor and a lawyer
  Sent Flo' Wyndham quickly then,
And removing her fine dinner,
  Waited patient for the men.
First the lawyer at the bedside
  Of poor Moses did appear;
And in answer to Flo's question,
  "Is he sane?" "Yes, very clear."

XLVIII.

"He desires to deed unto me
  All his wealth in lands and gold;
That in case of legal trouble,
  I his fortune vast may hold."
" Then this man you mean to marry?"
  "How else could I wear his name?"
" True; I beg your pardon, lady,
  Bring your witness, I'll remain."

XLIX.

" With my client." "Sir," addressing
  The starved sufferer on the couch,
"Do you wish to give your riches
  To this lady? Can you vouch
For her honesty, my dear sir?
  Will you deed her every bit
Of your gold?" "Yes," cried the poor wretch,
  "Und ten times more if I had it."

L.

"Are you sure you'll not repent you
  Of this action in one whit?
'Gain, will you give her all your riches?"
  "Yes, und more if I had it."
" Heavens I how the man must love you,"
  Said the learned man of law;
Then he read the legal papers,
  That he might repair each flaw.

LI.

Flo' Wyndham felt like laughing
  At the lawyer's words sincere,
But repressed the pert emotion,
  Not appearing him to hear.
Well, the deeds were signed, witnessed
  And given to the maid,
And Flo' Wyndham to the lawyer.
  With politeness thusly said :

LII.

" Sir, I thank you for your service,
  Soon I think my friend will rise
From this couch of sudden illness ;
  For suffering he doth despise.
Now, good-day, when e'er desired
  Is your service, I shall send,
And *remember 'tis your best plan
  To always be my friend.*"

LIII.

" Was there ever such an idiot?
  Here Miss Wyndham dares to claim

Herr Vanholstein's vast riches,
　　When not mentioned is her name.
Madame Flo' you're very foolish
　　This nonsense more to press
To his *wife*, and not betrothed
　　Are those documents addressed."

LIV.

Standing in a crowded court-room,
　　With Mrs. Briggs close at her side,
Was the maid whom Herr Vanholstein
　　Sought to make his bride.
Her little, aged companion,
　　Trembling, nervous stood ;
And on Flo's cheek fierce burning,
　　Glowed the fiery Spanish blood.

LV.

Turning to her small companion,
　　Flo' in ringing accents said :
" In disguise, adopted sister,
　　Long enough now have you staid."
From the head of the poor lady
　　Fell cap and false gray front,
From her eyes she took the glasses,
　　Then the bench she did confront.

LVI.

As she did, in amber billows
　　Fell her hair of shining gold
To her waist. FLORA VANHOLSTEIN
　　Clung to her sustainer bold.
" Mein frow comes here to mock me,

From her deep, deep grave;
Keeps her from me, keeps her from me,
  From her spirit's wrath me save,"

LVII.

Cried the wretched Greenvale miser;
  Then he turned away to fly,
But he fell, o'ercome with terror,
  'Mid horror's pangs to die.
Flo' looked on calm, untroubled,
  By the scene of wretched death;
And she smiled when Herr Vanholstein
  Drew his last o'er-tortured breath.

LVIII.

Then in tones of bugle clearness,
  The proud one her story told;
How she came to see her schoolmate,
  And the miser husband old.
Then she painted such a picture
  Of dark woe and despair,
Suffered by poor Flora,
  That no eye undimmed was there.

LIX.

Then, she said, with mischief gleamings
  Shooting from her dusky eyes:
" I contrived a scheme and cheated
  Moses out of his rich prize;
I drugged his wife and told him
  That his young bride was no more,
Whereupon he sought to win me;
  But as Blue Beard did of yore,

LX.

"He had met his match in cunning,
  I cajoled him with my wiles,
Till he'd do what e'er I asked him
  For a few electric smiles.
Believing that I'd wed him,
  To his wife he did secure
All his lands and goods, thus leaving
  Himself somehow very poor.

LXI.

"All this time his wife in disguise
  Remained beneath his roof;
If you wish, I can bring forward
  Other most excellent proof."
" No further proof is needed,"
  Said the judge, with smiling face,
As he gazed upon the Floras,
  Marking their peerless grace.

LXII.

Strangely fair and brilliant
  Were those two houries bright;
One as dark as Spanish lady, ·
  · One as Saxon princess bright.
Flora with her blue eyes shining
  Through a mist of happy tears,
Murmured : " Flo', my friend, my sister,
  Vanished now have all my fears;

LXIII.

" Never more need I to tremble
  With that strange, unholy dread."

" No, for now you are a widow,"
  And Flo' Wyndham shook her head.
Two months later Flo' was married
  To a gallant son of Mars,
Who had won, for daring actions,
  Flashing shoulder straps and stars.

LXIV.

And Flora, notwithstanding
  Her first experience so hard,
Gave her heart and hand and fortune
  To a noble-gifted bard ;
And together ever loving
  Dwells each Flora and her mate,
Blessed and happy, *seldom sighing*
  O'er Vanholstein's gloom-wrapt fate.

Falling Leaves.

I.

GENTLY passing, gently passing,
  Is the golden autumn dear,
And the leaves are falling, falling,
  From the branches brown and scar;
And as down they silent flutter,
  In their fall a voiceless woe
Seems to tell of long past pleasure,
  Joys forgotten years ago.

II.

As the leaves so mutely falling,
  Through the casement I behold;
Leaves that with the tempest sported,
  Leaves once crimson, green and gold;
Then methinks of fallen heroes,
  From their lofty pennons thrown,
Heroes like the great Napoleon,
  To whom fear was e'er unknown.

III.

Yes, the falling leaves are emblems
  Of that haughty, warlike one,
Who from sunny France's rulers,
  Snatched the proud, imperial throne;
Who defied the law of nations,

(126)

Scorning all that's true and good,
  Seeking fame and adulation
Till his soul was steeped in blood ;

IV.

Till the wreck of slaughtered legions,
  'Riched the dry and barren earth,
And the soil once grim and gory,
  To the winegrape now gives birth ;
Till the curse of hapless widows,
  Freighted more by orphans' tears,
Brought the wrath of God upon him,
  In the winter of his years.

V.

Thus the man who held a scepter,
  Seated on a lordly throne,
Lingered out his life remaining
  In a British prison lone ;
With no loving one to cheer him,
  Or to soothe his hours of pain ;
Oh, his life it must be weary,
  As he lay there crushed in chains.

VI.

Yes, the leaves so silent falling,
  Falling to the darksome earth ;
Flung from off the parent branches,
  Where kind nature gave them birth ;
Doth remind us of the weakness
  Of frail mortals here below,
And that naught but love and meekness,
  Us the realms of bliss can show.

The Dolly Varden Man.

I.

THERE are Dolly Varden dresses,
　That delight each lady's heart,
Dolly Varden hats and tresses,
　Greatest triumph of the art;
Every thing that's new is Varden,
　Be it bonnet, frock or fan;
But, girls, did you e'er encounter
　The true Dolly Varden Man?

II.

Do not start in well-bred wonder,
　The article is scarce, I know;
Few of our belles so charming,
　Can say, " He is my beau."
He is hard to find as diamonds
　Made after nature's primal plan;
Oh he is a God-sent blessing,
　This rare Dolly Varden Man.

III.

He is not a son of Mammon,
　All the gold is in his heart;
He is not the slave of fashion,

Kindness is the only art
To which he resorts, and honor
Marks this leader in life's van;
For the helpless and the friendless,
Trust the Dolly Varden Man.

IV.

You'll not know him by big seal rings
That on dandy fingers flash,
You'll not know him by sweet perfumes,
Or foppish show or dash;
Nor by tones so oft illusive,
Which so many triflers can
Use to cheat fond, trusting maidens—
The true Dolly Varden Man

V.

Scorns such ignoble conquests;
Once in life he wooes to wed;
Crowned with *sense*, and not *beavers*,
Is his noble, kingly head;
Friend and brother of the needy,
Oh, that every maiden can
Say with pride, " My lover truly
Is a Dolly Varden Man."

Love's Dying Plaint.

I.

Oh my heart is sadly breaking,
   Breaking with an anguished pain,
Never more can I recover
   My lost peace of mind again;
She was false and she was fickle,
   As the changing wind that blows;
But I loved the radiant beauty,
   Radiant as the royal rose.

II.

Pretended was her great love for me,
   Another heart held hers enthroned,
Within its depths, she toying coyly
   Taught me to call the gem my own.
Slave of her caprice, long I lingered
   At the cruel beauty's side,
And, no longer sane, I madly
   Pleaded her to be my bride.

III.

She laughed to scorn my passioned speeches,
   Angry flashed her azure eyes;
Bade me unlearn the love she taught me,
   Lessons that till death I'll prize.
For me life's dream of love is ended,

My heart is dying day by day,
My soul chafes in its mortal prison,
　　And pants from earth to flee away.

IV.

No longer shall I here a-linger,
　　To endure this cruel pain;
Never more shall I rejoicing
　　Breathe my vows to her again.
Oft I'm dreaming of the false love,
　　What time the young moon softly gleams,
'Luming earth and sky and river
　　With her silv'ry crescent beams.

V.

What time the flowers sweetly slumber
　　'Neath the azure-arching sky,
And the night-bird tender warbles
　　Serenades to his mate a-nigh;
And I dream of her as loving,
　　With a true, undying love,
Cheering me and gently guiding
　　Toward the realms of light above.

VI.

And my soul o'er-anguished yearns,
Yearns to soar unbound and free,
　　Through the mist of space, e'er watching,
False and fickle one, o'er thee;
　　For my heart is sadly breaking,
With a cruel, dying pain,
　　Oh never more can I recover
My sweet peace of mind again.

My Country Beau.

I.

A FARMER, yes he is, don't faint,
    The idea seems, I know,
Preposterous, that a belle like me
    Should have a country beau.

II.

But ere in anger you condemn
    Me as a silly girl,
For having thrown myself away,
    Upon a country churl ;—

III.

Remember that my heart was sick,
    And wearied to the core,
Of listening to the perfumed fops
    That courted me before.

IV.

They vowed they loved me more than life,
    Those brainless dandies gay,
But when they thought my wealth was gone,
    Like mists they passed away.

(132)

V.

My lawyer kind at my behest,
  The rumor circled round,
That in a speculation vast,
  My thousands all were drowned.

VI.

A district school I taught awhile,
  My ruse was sure you know,
For ere the golden Autumn came
  I met my country beau.

VII.

As through the fragrant fields one eve
  We roved, in accents low
He breathed forth his tale of love,
  My whole-souled country beau.

VIII.

Now, not for all the gifted men
  Your cities vain can show,
Would I exchange my heart's sole prince,
  My sun-bronzed country beau.

Beautiful Summer.

I.

O SUMMER! beautiful Summer,
   Once more thou art drawing near,
Brightest of all the seasons,
   Queen of the fast-flowing year;
In thy mantle of vernal richness,
   And crown of roses wine-red,
'Fore Sol, thine too ardent lover,
   Thou dost blushingly bow thy head.

II.

O Summer! beautiful Summer,
   Like many a maiden fair,
Thou dreamest not of the coming
   Autumn brown and sear;
To thee thy lover's fond glances
   Doth heaven's pure joys unfold,
But, Summer, they'll silver thy tresses,
   That are lighter than fairy-spuu gold.

III.

O Summer! beautiful Summer,
   In thy dreamy loveliness rare,
In the wealth of lilies and roses,

That are scattered everywhere;
In thy breath of perfumed sweetness,
    And voice of music low,
In thine eyes of lustrous splendor
    Is told a tale of woe.

IV.

And the tale is of short-lived pleasures,
    Of beauty whose reign is soon o'er,
Of how worthless are earth's richest pleasures,
    When we reach death's shadowy shore;
For wealth, nor beauty, nor greatness
    Can evade that last dread decree,
'Tis the soul's peerless beauty, unsullied
    By sin, that from us can not flee.

Departing Friends.

I.

THE golden Autumn days are here,
The saddest, brightest of the year;
   O'er earth a mantle brown,
Tinged with the rainbow's gorgeous dyes,
Glowing and beauteous from the skies,
   Is flung in grandeur down.

II.

The rose no longer proudly blooms,
Delightsome with her rich perfumes,
   Faded in beauty's prime;
The lily's royal head in death
Is bowed, and fled her fragrant breath,
   Sad proofs of fleeting time.

III.

The feathered songsters in the grove,
Breathe forth their farewell songs of love;
   They love their northern home,
And soon afar in favored lands,
Untouched by Winter's freezing hands,
   Rejoicing they will roam.

IV.

The glowing tints the woods display,
Foreshadow naught but fell decay;
   The brightest skies of Autumn morn,
Though blue as Lerna's crystal breast,

(130)

And bright as Jove's bejeweled crest,
  Are harbingers of storm.

V.

When warbling birds and fragrant flowers,
And vines that gem my summer bowers,
  Are from my vis.on flown,—
The sole companions of my life;
How shall I face its daily strife,
  Unaided and alone?

VI.

Alone, no friends but these have I,
For in them Hope and Faith I spy
  The friends that nature gives;
And in her friends I see the sign
Of God who promised rest divine,
  To those who trusting lives.

VII.

Deserted by them I bemoan
My fate, and yearn with them to roam
  Where summer reigns in beauty.
The bravest heart when lonely left,
Of kindred friends and joy bereft,
  Breaks while it does its duty.

VIII.

But this alone keeps from despair,
The heart o'er-wrought by grievous care;
  When life's wild storms are over,
Beyond this vale of falling tears,
When Time has sped a few short years,
  Heaven's joys await the rover.

Be Brave.

I.

WHEN fickle fortune grimly frowns
  On you, her mortal devotee,
And crushes 'neath her cruel wheel,
  Your dreams of great prosperity,—
Never falter, never quail,
Coward hearts are sure to fail.

II.

When glowing hopes of future joys
  Are scattered like autumnal leaves
Before your eager, anxious eyes,
  And leaves you o'er their wreck to grieve,—
Never falter, never wait,
Coward hearts are never great.

III.

When smiling friends of summer flee,
  The moment sorrows o'er you sweep,
Grieve not because they've proven false;
  Nay, rather smile instead of weep,
And bravely face life's work anew,
For sunshine friends are never true.

IV.

When Death doth spread his sable wing
  Above your mansion, thence to bear
The treasured darlings of your heart
  Unto the Father, weep nor fear,
For he will guard each blossom rare,
And you in turn their joys will share.

V.

Be true to God and to yourself,
  Be brave of heart and strong of hand,
Whatever cross or woe he sends,
  Is but to test his chosen band;
Then fight 'gainst wrong to win the right,
And wear a crown of glory bright.

Spring.

I.

ONCE again the leaves are budding,
  Once again the flowerets blow
In their robes of beauteous rose-hue,
  Perfumed orchards sweetly glow.

II.

Once again the grass is growing,
  Emerald carpet of the earth,
And the merry, wild-wood songsters
  Fill the air with joy and mirth.

III.

Now the joyous, laughing streamlet,
  Bounds exultant on its way;
Freed from nature's icy bondage,
  By the smiling god of day.

IV.

Once again the lambs are bleating,
  The lowing herds at evening tide,
Give to Spring a welcome greeting,
  By the murmuring river's side.

(140)

V.

Yes, 'tis Spring, the morn of seasons,
    Dawning of a glad, new life;.
Making earth appear an Eden,
    Everything with pleasure rife.

VI.

Once again; ah! we may never
    More rejoice that Spring is here;
Let us revel in her beauties,
    Radiant morning of the year.

VII.

But beyond this world of shadows,
    Where 'tis said the angels sing,
We may find eternal pleasure,
    Find a never-ending SPRING.

Despair Not.

I.

DESPAIR not, my brother,
  Though dark seems the hour,
Thy fate rests with Him,
  The great Father of power;
Then turn not faint-hearted
  From thy hard task away,
But remember 'tis darkest
  Ere dawns the bright day.

II.

Despair not when tempests
  Thy frail bark besets,
When the black waves of sorrow
  Submerge it in depths
Of bitterest anguish;
  Be hopeful and pray,
And remember 'tis darkest
  Ere dawns the bright day.

III.

When hearts we deemed true,
  Have false proven and flown,
And leave us to battle

Life's warfare alone;
Mourn not o'er the lost loves,
Be cheerful and gay,
For remember 'tis darkest
Ere dawns the bright day.

IV.

Despair not, though Death,
With his merciless dart,
Should pierce to the core,
Some fond, trusting heart;
He will cherish each spirit,
And when done is thy day,
Thou'lt learn that 'tis darkest
Ere dawns the bright day.

V.

Put your faith and your hope
And your true love in God,
For he gives us strength.
To pass under his rod;
For though deep is the gloom,
Still we see a faint ray
That tells us 'tis darkest
Ere dawns the bright day.

Maidens Deck the Soldiers' Graves

I.

'TIS a tribute of love from true Christians,
  To strew each lone, verdant bed
With flowers fresh, fragrant and glowing,
  'Tis honor due unto the dead
Heroes that fought 'neath the standard
  Of glorious red, white and blue,
All fearless of Death and his terrors,
  So gallant, so dauntless, so true.

II.

They gave their hearts' blood to defend it,
  The banner of freedom so grand,
Nor wept when they left the dear loved ones,
  With saber and rifle in hand;
They quailed not when war's deadly thunders
  Shook the earth with its terrific roar;
For their country they gloried in dying,
  For HER drenched the sod with their gore.

III.

Full many a gallant young soldier,
  Brave sons of the great war-god Mars,
Lie friendless, unwept and uncared for,

'Neath heaven's bright sentinel stars ;
O'er these, ye maidens angelic,
  Shed sympathy's tenderest tears,
Strew the lone graves with bright garlands,
  Your reward will come in future years.

IV.

Then strew ye the graves of our soldiers,
  And strew ye each lone, mossy bed,
With flowers fresh, fragrant and glowing,
  The tribute is due to the dead
Heroes that fought 'neath the standard
  Of glorious red, white and blue,
All fearless of Death and his terrors,
  So gallant, so dauntless, so true.

Have Charity.

I.

Pause, my brother, why should we
    Pass the orphan by unheeded?
Why, what has he done to thee,
    That such cruel words are meted
Out to the poor orphan boy,
'Neath yon darkly frowning sky?

II.

A beggar, yes; whose fault? not his,
    For it thou'lt not leave him starving,
Surely thou a mite will give;
    Heavens! think of thine own darling,
Suffering hunger, suffering cold,
The anguish of which ne'er was told.

III.

A thief perchance, who made him so?
    Want, an iron-handed master,
When the rich man bids him go,
    Then this demon holds him faster;
Die he will not, live he will,
Have mercy nor his poor soul kill.

IV.

Right, my brother, God will bless thee
For this one act of kindness;
See the poor boy feebly press
Thy hands and brush away the blindness
From his eyes, bright, grateful tears,
The first he may have shed for years.

V.

There, my boy, accept this mite,
˙Small in sooth; yet if each Christian
Would contribute such a tithe
To the orphans, what a vision
Of rejoicing would appear,
Where now all is dark and *drear*.

A Question and Answer.

I.

QUEEN LILYBELLE of Flora's court,
Who loves her robes of snow to sport,
Once glancing at a violet blue,
Exclaimed: "You're poor and simple too;
Why don't you dress in robes of white,
Pure as the moon's rare, silver light?
Why don't you hold your head on high,
That you may see what's passing by,
Nor linger there, drooping and low,
Where of the world naught you can know?"

II.

"Because," the violet meek replied,
"My Maker made me without pride;
A lowly, humble flower am I,
While you were bred to hold on high
Your beauteous head like diademed queen;
By rude, refined you may be seen;
The unfeeling of your sweets may taste,
Then onward press with cruel haste;
The thoughtless and the sin-stained too
May pause your beauty rare to view.

(148)

The lurid sun sips fiercely all
The dew that in your heart doth fall ;
You're doomed to fall and swift decay,
Your beauty lingers but a day.

III.

While I low nestling in the grass,
Escape the vulgar as they pass ;
Nor can the sun sip up the dew
That cooling gems my breast so blue.
I live content with what I've got,
Grateful to God for this my lot;
Nor covet that to others given,
For which I'll bloom again in heaven.

ope.

I.

BRIGHT star, clearly shining,
　To illumine our way,
When darkness and sorrow
　　Sweeps o'er us;
Resplendent thy luster and
　Peerless thy ray,
Ever gloriously blazing
　　Before us.

II.

Hope, beauteous deceiver
　Of trusting mankind,
Were it not for thy mystic
　　Encoring,
In idle abandon would slumber
　The mind,
Proud genius and talent
　　Ignoring.

III.

Thy presence to life
　Fans ambition's proud flame,
And arouses the soul's
　　Best endeavors;

(150)

Thy votary untiring doth
  Toil to win fame,
Till the harvest of victory
  He gathers.

IV.

Some call thee of life
  The sole arrant bane,
A chimera shapeless,
    And shallow;
But what would be earth
  Were it not for thy reign;
Hope, every true man
    Thy name hallows.

V.

The young hopes for pleasure,
  The toiler success,
The aged for repose at death's
    Portals;
The soldier for Fame's sanguine
  Glory-dyed crest,
And the dying, joy with
    The immortals.

VI.

Then let us hope on, radiant star,
  Never vail
Thy luster from those thou
    Art cheering,
But shine on a bright
  Beacon,
Through tempest and gale, till we reach
    That bright port we are nearing.

There is Poetry in Autumn.

I.

THERE is poetry in Autumn,
    In the softly falling leaves,
In the song of merry wild birds,
    As they flutter 'mong the trees;
In the rippling of the streamlet,
    In the setting of the sun,
In the mists that from the valleys
    Float in clouds of vapor dun.

II.

There is poetry in Autumn,
    When the farmer proudly gleans
The fruits of months of labor,
    When he stores the golden grains;
When he plucks the purple wine grape,
    And the apples golden, russet, red;
When he thanks the God of nature
    For the blessings on him shed.

III.

There is poetry in Autumn,
    When we through the woodlands rove,
In each brier, shrub and thicket,
    In each flaming maple grove,
In the robes of gold and purple,

That each forest king doth wear;
In the clinging moss so verdant,
   In the meadows brown and sear.

IV.

There is poetry in Autumn,
   In the squirrel blithe and gay,
Who 'mid mirth-provoking antics,
   Hides his winter store away;
In the lads that go a-nutting,
   Feet and faces brown and bare,
In the lasses gayly decking
   With berries red their wealth of hair.

V.

There is poetry in Autumn,
   And it thrills my soul to see
All nature joyous offering
   Homage to the Deity;
Then shall man alone be grateless
   For the gifts to him outpoured,
Nor prostrate him in thanksgiving
   To Jehovah, nature's Lord?

Spring Flowers.

I.

BUTTERCUPS and daisies,
    Little gems of light,
Peeping through the mosses,
    Gold and pearly white.

II.

Primroses and violets,
    Emblems of guileless youth;
Innocence and virtue,
    Tender, loving truth.

III.

Bluebells bright and cowslips
    Deck the meadows green,
Sweetest little floral stars
    That in spring are seen.

IV.

When the sun is highest
    In each perfumed heart,
A bright dew-drop lingers,
    As if loth to part—

V.

From its chosen blossom;
  As it fain would keep
The fragile thing from danger,
  Waking or asleep.

VI.

Thus our guardian angel
  · Hovers loving nigh,
Shielding us from danger
  Till we reach our home on high.

The Abode of the Muses.

I.

For months I've been searching
  In fancy, now mind,
Maps, atlases, histories,
  Endeavoring to find
The court of the Muses;
  All vainly I sought,
With pitiful failure
  My searching was fraught.

II.

To the heights of Parnassus
  At first I repaired,
Where the nine peerless ladies
  Were tutored and reared;
But never a one of the Nine did I see,
  Near the fount of Hyppocrene,
Bright, gushing and free.

II.

Apollo, their sovereign,
  Was nowhere in sight,
And Pegasus' winged charger,
  Had taken his flight;
All gloom-wrapt and dreary

(156)

Looked mountain and lea,
And mourning and weary,
  Low sobbed the dark sea.

IV.

Disappointed, half angry,
  'I turned me away,
Nor heeded the sparkle
  Of Aganippe's spray ;
And straight to Mt. Ida
  My course then I steered,
Where Jupiter Ammon
  Was fostered and reared.

V.

For foolish and poet-like,
  Joyous methought
That there I'd discover
  What long I had sought ;
The mountain so sacred,
  So wondrously famed,
The hill where Amalthea
  Great Jove had sustained—

VI.

Where the Corybantes
  Had guarded their king
From the jaws of the father.
  'Mid dire suffering
I reached in due season,
  Unaided, unknown,
To find that my Muses
  Far from me had flown.

VII.

To the island of Delos
    I pointed my course,
Resolved to discover
    My ladies perforce ;
To the home of Latona
    My fancy did fly,
The birthplace of deities,
    Sacred and high.

VIII.

Where Diana of chastity,
    Goddess and queen,
Watched over Apollo
    With sisterly mien,
And thwarted fierce Juno's
    Revengeful design,
And rules o'er the hunter
    With smiling benign.

IX.

I searched the fair island,
    Hill, valley and cover,
But never a Muse
    Did poor fancy discover.
The Synagogues Jewish,
    The temples of Ind,
The shrines of fell Gunga,
    And Bowanee's the fiend—

X.

I searched half despairing,
    But nothing was there :

No, the Muses coquettish,
    Were acting unfair.
Then Egypt's dark pyramids
★ Lured one to come,
St. Peter's Cathedral
    Me welcomed to Rome.

XI.

Catacombs, vestry, hall,
    Palace and tomb,
Mosque, forest and valley,
    In sunlight and gloom,
I searched long and patient,
    All vain 'twas alack,
To me my fair Muses
    Failed e'er to come back.

XII.

Great, great was the chagrin
    I silent endured,
The spook of ambition
    Felt highly injured;
To find their retreat
    By false means or fair,
Was my resolve, in
    Which fancy took share.

XIII.

Oh, how these gay Muses
    In sport must have laughed
As the nectar of poetry
    Daily they quaffed ;
But I was in earnest,

To Greece I returned,
Where Troy, famous city,
  Was pillaged and burned.

XIV.

'Mid the ruins I wandered,
  In awe I reviewed,
Through the vista of ages,
  The war steed of wood;
In whose hollow body
  The Greeks were concealed,
Who opened the gates
  And Troy's secrets revealed.

XV.

I gazed upon Helen,
  The spoiler of Troy;
By her charms all excelling,
  Paris she decoyed;
And Hector avenging
  The wrong, lowly fell;
In Elysium, the heaven
  Where ancient gods dwell,

XVI.

'Tis said that the hero
  Of Homer resides;
Let no sedate Christians
  The saying deride.
But vain was my voyage,
  No Muse lingered there,
And I vowed to pursue them
  Through sea, sky and air.

XVII.

To the mines of Siberia,
    Relentless I hied,
But alas for my ardor,
    With anguish I cried ;
My furs I'd forgotten,
    My garments were thin,
The ice and the tempests
    They ruthless let in.

XVIII.

My teeth were a-chatter,
    My face it was blue,
Cold as Hecate's heart,
    My benumbed limbs grew.
The Muses I hated,
    For what? their fell pride ;
And but for Sol's warmth,
    I think I had died.

XIX.

They may have been there,
    I'm not positive now,
For I fled from that region,
    Well, I can not tell how ;
I encountered no Muse
    On the frost-bestrewn track,
To the realms of heat,
    With joy I flew back.

XX.

At length, sad and weary,

11

I faced my dear home,
　Unrewarded and dreary,
　　All joyless and lone ;
And I wept from sheer anger,
　To think I was foiled,
That for naught I had traveled,
　　Schemed, struggled and toiled.

XXI.

When home I returned,
　With dull, leaden heart,
To my friend, the Professor,
　I flew to impart
The miserable tidings ;—
　All smiling he heard,
No chord of kind pity
　　My wretched tale stirred.

XXII.

" Professor, you're heartless,"
　Indignant I cried,
" With eyes if not tongue,
　All my woes you deride."
He laughed at my anger,
　Then kindly he said :
" Just listen one moment,
　　Nay, shake not your head ;

XXIII.

" 'Tis the error of many,"
　He smiling went on,
" To chase after fancies,
　Then find them all gone ;

They travel, vain seeking,
　In Asia and Rome,
What, if they but knew it,
　Is always at home."

XXIV.

He opened a chamber,
　Rich was its design,
Wherein sat the peerless,
　The immortal Nine ;
I gazed unbelieving,
　But found it was so,
And I ne'er have ceased thanking
　Good Prof. Rippetoe.

The Fenian Exile's Resolve.

I.

I AM a son of Erin fair,
    And proudly do I claim
Her as the brightest heritage,
    Queen of unrivaled fame—
Land of my birth, my boyhood's home,
    Far o'er the tossing main,
With breaking heart I sadly roam,
    Devoid of friend or name.

II.

Banished from thee, my native isle,
    A fugitive I've flown,
Loosed by a friendly turnkey,
    An exile doomed to roam;
Because I loved my country best,
    Defied the Saxon's power,
As many a hero, good and great,
    Defied that curse before.

III.

A Fenian, yes, I joined that band
    Of brothers brave, to fight
For Erin; to rend her chains,

And chase away the night
Of bondage, that, like thunder cloud,
  Hung o'er our isle so green,
Until God's glorious sunburst breaks
  O'er her in golden sheen.

IV.

Until the blood of EMMET shed,
  By Britons' ruthless hands,
Is thrice ten thousand times avenged
  By Erin's noblest sons;
Until the flag of emerald green,
  Floats ne'er more to come down,
O'er ocean's wave, o'er peasant's hut,
  O'er ruins gray, long brown.

V.

Think ye the spirits of the dead
  . Heroes that's passed away,
Rest peaceful in their lonesome graves,
  While o'er their hallowed clay,
Doth pass the feet of *cringing slaves*,
  Who wear the Saxon yoke,
Nor *dare* their masters to enrage
  By one AVENGING STROKE?

VI.

Think, brothers, of our isle so green,
  Think of her maids so fair,
Whose eyes excel the heaven's deep blue,
  And their bright, waving hair;
Think of them as they nurture *slaves*
  Upon their breasts so pure;

And while ye think, ask of your hearts,
  " Must *we* this e'er endure ? "

VII.

No, by the faith our fathers loved,
  No, by all-holy power,
No, by the blood of brave hearts shed,
  In England's gloomy towers,
Her daughters shall not nurture *slaves*
  Much longer, soon the day
Will come when thousands swords will gleam
  To sweep our foes away.

VIII.

We'll wash in blood from Irish soil,
  Cursed slavery's darksome stain,
And drive our foemen in the sea,
  As 'fore we drove the Dane ;
As Fingal brave made Citric's **grave**,
  Deep in the watery main ;
Together we will fight or fall,
  Till Ireland's free again.

IX.

Then, Fenian brothers, let us join
  Our vows with one accord,
To sweep from Erin's lovely isle
  The red-coat and the lord ;
And with our trust in God on high,
  Who rules all earthly things,
We'll battle bravely till our isle,
  NO MORE IS SLAVE OF KINGS !

To Mrs. Mary Helm.

I.

DEAR friend of mine, fain would I breathe
  In words the gratitude I bear,
But though of womankind, my tongue
  Would sadly fail me then I fear ;
So pen and muse must do the task,
  And blithely sing a little lay,
A tribute that thou wilt accept,
  Sincerely from my soul I pray.

II.

For when I needed one to guide
  The fiery steed Pegasus straight,
Say, was't not thou who held the reins
  Of Fancy pointing to the gate
Of bright success to which I turned ?
  And aided by thy words of cheer,
Kept bravely on and gladly learned
  The value of thy wisdom dear.

III.

And was it not thy merry smile,
  That chased all lurking doubts away
From me a timid woman-child,
  Yielding to influences' sway ;

Now sad, now bright,
    Jūst as the light rains
Dim the skies of April day?

IV.

And when my days of toil were done,
    With many a wise and timely word,
Thou badest me guard the prize I won;
    For simple as a half-fledged bird,
I longed to try my pinions gay,
    And flutter through the world so wide;
But gently saidst thou : "Alice May,
    Let good Dame Prudence be thy guide."

V.

And so I shall, but thou, kind friend,
    Must watch the dame, for prudish girls
Are *very nice*, that much I claim,
    But truly happy ones are pearls ;
I won't be prudish ; that's too much ;
    But following in THY FOOTSTEPS PROUD,
I'll live and learn and love as such
    That 'neath no grievous cares are bowed.

VI.

So now, good-by, that is in rhyme,
    For every day we're sure to meet,
While for us Fate a thread of time
    Doth spin along Life's busy street;
And while I live, I'll love thee all,
    That one like me with reverence can,
While doing all my duties sweet,
    And maturing my life's bright plan.

To Jas. C. C. Holenshade, Esq.,

I.

FRIEND of woman's sure advancement,
  Friend of genius in her born,
To make bright her life of study,
  Thou thy college hath adorned;
'Neath thy roof to toil is pleasure,
  Heart and brain doth there expand,
All the Muses there are treasured
  By thy noble, generous hand. `

II.

Euterpe, goddess of sweet music,
  Tunes her sad harp and guitar,
There the organ 'neath her fingers
  Swells triumphant; near and far
Are its notes so mellow floating,
  While piano-forte rich, rare,
Fills with strains that seem of heaven,
  All the flower-beperfumed air.

III.

Clio, Calliope and Erato,
  With sweet Euterpe doth preside
(169)

In thy college, o'er the gifted
　　Ones that 'neath its roof reside;
Polhymnia, Melpomene,
　　Terpsichore Thalia sings and **dances,**
Dreams and lectures
　　In thy palace day by day;

IV.

In the flashing of the fountain,
　　In the sparkle of its spray,
In the ripple of the lakelet,
　　In the fishes sporting gay;
In the vernal, velvet, sloping
　　Lawn, begemmed with Flora's **bloom,**
In the air so soft and balmy,
　　In the flowers' rich perfume,

V.

Dwells the proof of all thy labor,
　　Woman's generous friend and **kind;**
Oh! how can she ever thank thee,
　　Thou enricher of her mind;
May her prayers for thy long-living,
　　That thy joys may have increase,
That to thee she'll prove a blessing,
　　Be heard by the Prince of peace.

To Annie Hofher Gorious.

I.

Last Thursday morn, as jovial Sol
　　Mounted his car of gold on high,
To make his circuit round the earth,
　　A festive scene greeted his eye,
As through the chapel windows he
　　Allowed his golden rays to pour;
There at the altar silent, grave,
　　The god beheld a group of four.

II.

The bride and bridegroom hand in hand,
　　Before the priest low, reverent bowed,
The bridesmaid and the groomsman stand
　　With looks half fearful and half proud;
The words that joined the two in one
　　Were spoken, and the blessings said,
Fond, loving friends were gathered there,
　　To smile upon the newly wed.

III.

The day god smiled upon the bride,
　　He kissed the softly blushing cheek,
For he resolved no cloud should come

(171)

To cause that loving one to weep ;
He smiled when from her parents dear,
    The bridegroom bore her w th proud hea .
Her tender sighs were not of fear,
    The tears were joyous which she shed.

IV.

Then may the future for her be
    As bright and cloudless as the day
When Sol, in all his brill ancy,
    Illumed the vaulted, milky way ;
May flowers of hope and love divine,
    Bestrew the path o'er which she treads,
And Heaven's blessing rare, sublime,
    Rest quietly on her youthful head.

To Jennie Crawford Davis.

I.

So, Jennie, thou'rt wedded,
   And ended's the span
Of thy maidenhood joyous,
   At thy birth which began;
Thou'rt happy, I know it,
   By the blush on thy cheeks,
And thy bright eyes soft glowing,
   That with eloquence speaks.

II.

We are glad and we're sorry,
   That for thee is o'er
Thy girlhood days merry;
   Alas! and no more
Canst thou join our frolics,
   For chained fast for life,
Art thou, dearest Jennie,
   Since becoming a wife.

III.

Well, Jennie, be happy,
   And never complain,
But let thy heart beat

(173)

To the silver refrain
Of love and contentment;
Be blithesome and free,
For the love of thy schoolmates
Is ever with thee.

IV.

And may Heaven's rare blessings,
Mystic divine,
Rest like a bright halo
On that young head of thine;
And may the dear partner
Thou hast chosen for life,
Be a comfort and joy
To his lovely young wife.

To Jennie Roots Thompson.

I.

YES, Jennie, friend of mine, thou'rt wed,
  Hymen hath claimed thee for his own,
Thy maiden days fore'er are fled,
  To love's sweet kingdom thou hast flown;
Upon thy brow the orange blooms
  Were gleaming like a pearly crown, .
Exhaling forth a rare perfume,
  Sweeter than frankincense renowned.

II.

When he, the lord of thy young heart,
  To thee 'fore God and man was bound
By silken bonds inwrought with gold,
  The purest that in heaven is found;
Upon thy cheek the roses glowed,
  The love-light in thine eyes was seen,
As bending 'fore the man of God,
  Thou gavest to him thy heart serene.

III.

Light was that heart when from the home
  Of childhood by him thou wert borne,
Thy bridegroom's love was all thine own,
  Thy tears spoke not of souls that mourn;
Pure joy was thine, and may thy life
  Be peaceful, blissful as the day
When he, thy love, first called thee wife,
  And won thy trusting heart away.

(175)

The Magic Gift.

I.

THERE is a gift which mortals prize
   Far more than priceless Orient gems,
'Tis given to the gay, the wise,
   To peasants ; kings with diadems
Stoop from their thrones to taste its sweets ;
   They pine, without it languish, die,
Or sordid cruel, heartless grow,
   If Fate the gift to them deny.

II.

Parent of all in man that's good,
   Dark is the soul that holds it not,
The human heart's life-giving food,
   With wondrous magic power 'tis fraught ;
It warms the miser cold to life,
   It melts the pitiless heart of stone,
It changes darkness into light,
   Brings joy where sorrow e'er is known.

III.

It gems the cheek of maidenhood,
   With blushings from the royal rose,
And heavy eyes with tears bedewed,

Bright flashes with its mystic glows;
It vails our faults with rosy leaves,
   And brings rich beauty to the plain,
The guilt-stained heart repentant heaves,
   For it swift turns to God again.

IV.

With fetters wrought of silk and gold,
   It chains fond hearts together fast,
Nor lets them sunder that sweet tie,
   Till life's brief waiting span is past.
Ah, what is it? you breathless ask,
   That can so strangely powerful prove,
I'll answer, friends, triumphant that,
   'Tis deathless, heaven-born, loyal love.

In Memoriam.

(179)

A. P. Newkirk, Esq.

I.

He has flown from our presence,
   Beloved of the Muses,
That reign o'er the souls of
     True poets through time;
They mourn o'er his ashes,
   The sad tear suffuses
Their orbs of rare luster
     And beauty sublime.

II.

They loved him, our Azel!
   His mind of great promise
Was stored with rich thoughts
     That from Helicon flow;
They honored their subject,
   With gifts all excelling,
For they deemed he a star
     Literary would glow.

III.

From the heights of Parnassus
   The immortal Nine watched,
Guarding their treasure ;

(181)

While gloriously
They sought to inspire his soul
With an ardor
As warm as the loves
Of the fabled Peri,

IV.

That charms all the lords
Of the far sunny Orient;
(Her beauty in human
None ever could see)
As lavish their gifts, as the
Waves of Hyppocrene,
That ripples bright gushing
In fetterless glee.

V.

From 'neath the gold hoofs
Of Pegasus, winged charger,
As glides the broad tides
Of the blue ocean free,
They crowned him with genius,
This pet of the Muses;
Calliope of eloquence, goddess and queen,
Yielded her wealth;

VI.

Till with soul-stirring pathos
His voice would excite
Every sympathy keen
That lurked in the breast
Of the dullest of mortals;
And when to poesy he chose to incline,

With magic-like power
  He would ope the soul's portals,
To mirth tender sadness,
  Or sweet love sublime.

VII.

And who that e'er knew him,
  But felt the attractions
Of numberless beauties,
  That to his mind clung;
The gayety, wit and free
  Spirit, thoughts matchless,
That like laurel garlands
  Around his brows hung.

VIII.

At home and abroad,
  Ever gay and light-hearted,
He thought not to toil
  For the world's rich pelf,
But lived fondly dreaming,
  Nor heeded the passage
Of years, both forgetful
  Of time and himself.

IX.

He died in the vigor
  Of noble young manhood,
Afar from those that would
  Love and defend ;
Grim mystery shrouds
  In a mantle of shadow,

The fate of our countryman,
    Brother and friend.

X.

But who that hath lost
    A beloved son or brother,
Can repress a deep sigh,
    Or pity's sad tear ;
Oh, who but sore grieved
    For the silver-haired mother,
As she drooped o'er her Azel's
    Dark funereal bier.

XI.

He is gone ; 'neath the sod
    His pulseless heart slumbers,
Forgotten by strangers,
    His sorrowful fate;
But the poet, sad-hearted,
    In mournful numbers,
The tale of his worth
    And high genius relates.

XII.

As a star that in glory
    Arises at evening,
Through the dusk brow of heaven,
    Triumphant it hies;
When *lo*, from the north
    Comes the tempest-cloud driven
By fierce howling winds,
    That career through the skies.

XIII.

The gloomy vail hides
  Its but half revealed splendor,
And darkness supreme,
    O'er the vast expanse reigns;
The storm spirit *ruthless*
  Its ray doth extinguish,
And Nature thus robbed
    Of her treasure, remains

XIV.

Shrouded in darkness,
  Despairingly mourning,
While fast fall her tears
    As the bright summer rain,
Nor dreams of the light
  That must so n be returning,
With Hope, Heaven's balm,
    To assuage all her pains.

XV.

Thus vanished our friend,
  From the home of the mortals;
Death cruel extinguished
    His soul's ardent fire,
Blasting the hopes that
  Cheer on to Fame's portals,
And stilling forever
    His musical lyre.

XVI.

But, Azel, beyond
  This vale woe-beshadowed,

In that bright spirit land
    Where 'tis said angels dwell,
Thy friends hope to meet thee,
    Rejoicing and hallowed,
Chanting praise unto Him
    Who doeth all things well.

Miss Amy Gilchrist.

I.

THOU hast vanished from our presence,
    Amy dear, devoted friend,
For thee in youth's bright morning,
    Fleeting Time attained his end;
Closed on earth are thy tender eyes,
    Thy voice we'll hear no more,
But triumphantly thou'rt chanting
    Hymns on heaven's mystical shore.

II.

Bending 'fore the throne of Jesus,
    Father, Spirit, martyred Son,
Thou art praising him who gloriously
    Our souls' redemption won.
On thy brow the saints' bright halo,
    Resplendently doth shine,
Nor sin nor sorrow e'er can dim
    Or mar thy bliss divine.

III.

Often, Amy, I am dreaming,
    Gently dreaming, friend, of thee,
What time the moon is softly gleaming

O'er the lonesome hill and lea,
What time the spirit tender whispers
- Of the mystic home beyond,
Where the dear departed loved ones,
Are watching, waiting fond.

IV.

And I dream of thee as smiling
O'er the troubles of this life,
Of thine influence as aiding
Thy beloved through earthly strife;
And I know that thou art waiting
Parents, sisters, kindred friends,
At heaven's radiant portals,
Where all spirit struggle ends.

Miss Mary Loftus.

I.

SHE is not dead, but calmly sleeping,
  The last long sleep that mortals know,
While parents fond are sadly weeping,
  And moaning: "Oh, why did she go?"
A mother's heart is slowly breaking,
  A father's tears in silence flow,
Brothers strong with grief are chafing,
  'Neath anguish keen their-heads doth bow.

II.

But she, beloved by all that knew her,
  Now mingles with Christ's spotless fold;
The face of our loved, blessed Savior,
  'Tis her pure joy now to behold;
A halo of unfading glory,
  Her angel brows softly entwine,
And harping with the heavenly harpers,
  She smiling bows 'fore Jesus' shrine.

III.

She was a daughter dutiful,
  With spirit gentle, mild and meek,
And from her life we blossoms cull,

Breathing of innocence most sweet;
She passed from midst us like a flower,
Touched by the chilling breath of frost,
Fading unseen until the hour
When loving hearts knew she was lost.

IV.

Lost to this world of endless sorrow,
Restored to heaven, from whence she came;
For Death, the Reaper of the flowers,
Bore back to Christ her spirit's flame;
But thou, O God, remember those
From whom thou hast reclaimed thine own,
Send thou from heaven a balm to soothe
The hearts where Woe her seeds hath sown.

Miss Amanda Scofield.

I.

Oh! Amanda, oh! Amanda,
  Long departed sister dear,
Can thy spirit bright remember
  All the friends and loved ones dear?
Can it watch far through the vistas
  Of blue, mystic, boundless space,
Marking all our earthly actions,
  From that high and holy place?

II.

Oh! Amanda, oh! Amanda,
  Bright and spotless child of God,
Bitter were our hearts' repinings,
  As we bowed beneath his rod;
When the Reaper of the flowers,
  Bore thee from those loving here,
Unto Him who reigns in glory,
  Lord of heaven's resplendent sphere.

III.

Oh! Amanda, oh! Amanda,
  Dwelling in the courts of love,
Chanting praises to the Savior,
  Who left his throne above;
To atone unto the Father

(191)

For a world; that world to save
From the depths of fearful sorrow,
And the soul from Folly's grave.

IV.

Wilt thou watch and wait our coming?
Wilt thou greet us at the gate,
Where alike the poor and lowly
Enter with the rich and great?
Wilt thou, by some angel power,
Tell us when the day is nigh,
That the angel of the shadow,
Is to bear our souls on high?

V.

Fare thee well, beloved sister,
Gentle daughter, loving friend,
All who knew thee in thy lifetime,
Hope to meet thee when the end
Of Time for them hath vanished,
To the strange and buried past;
And solved are heaven's secrets,
By their eager souls at last.

VI.

Fare thee well, no longer mourning
Bitterly, rebellious, sad,
Are the hearts of thy beloved ones,
But to hope's refrain so glad;
Father's, mother's, sister's, brother's
Hearts are keeping happy time,
For they deem erelong to meet thee,
In the realms of bliss sublime.

Henry the Eighth.

I.

BRITANNIA is a lovely land,
  Her castles bold are old and hoary,
For in them ruled with lordly hand,
And serfs low bowed 'neath their command,
  Full many a knight in feudal glory.

II.

Britannia's bards are lofty famed,
  And prone to sing their monarch's praises,
Who in the by-gone ages reigned,
When kings *were men*, and seldom feigned
  False sentiments in act or phrases.

III.

Britannia's kings were royal born,
  And bred to rule that lovely nation,
And never was a Tudor head
Bowed 'neath the weight of cruel dread,
  That haunt most men of lofty station.

IV.

'Twas thus it happened that while reigned
  A glorious line of Tudor princes,
Fair Albion grew beloved and famed,

Her fiercest subjects all were tamed,
 Their statesmanship this plain evinces.

V.

The Tudors were a famous line,
 They all were learned and noble-hearted,
Until 'twas willed by Fate and Time,
To change their virtues into crime;
 To Henry the Eighth this was imparted.

VI.

Now Henry the Eighth who wore the crown
 Of Albion, was, so Shakespeare tells us,
A man for love and war renowned,
When wealth and beauty did abound,
 And likewise he was fiercely jealous.

VII.

No sooner did he mount the throne,
 Left to him by his predecessors,
Than Arragon's fair princess, known
As Catherine, became his own,
 With all her beauty, love and treasures.

VIII.

For years he lived and loved his queen,
 With all his husband fondness tender,
And England's life was calm, serene;
He ruled and wrote, grand was his mien,
 Till he was styled the faith's defender.

IX.

But man is man despite the say

Of sage that he can rule his feeling;
For on a direful, fatal day,
The king succumbed to Anne's sway,
 And at her feet full soon was kneeling.

X.

The Siren used her every art,
 To hold in thrall her royal lover;
'Neath Cupid's lash she made him smart,
The king and queen she vowed to part,
 And that 'neath honor's golden cover.

XI.

The days crept by on leaden wings,
 Sweet Anne was enchanting, charming,
And Henry, 'mid dire sufferings
Of heart and mind and conscience stings
 Was prey to love and fear alarming.

XII.

He hated Catherine with a hate
 That well might melt an iceberg chilly;
Old, ugly, what meant cruel Fate,
By binding him in wedded state,
 To one who suited him so illy?

XIII.

For days he pondered in and out,
 He loved fair Boleyn to distraction,
Their marriage must be brought about;
But then beyond the slightest doubt,
 His queen would fain oppose the action.

XIV.

At length, although of royal birth,
   The highest man in all the nation,
He stooped to ask assistance worth
Far more than gold, of one whom earth
   Regarded as of lowly station;

XV.

Thus proving that, beyond a doubt,
   Kings are like any other mortals;
With evil failings, sins about
As many as the lowest lout,
   That dwells within our cottage portals.

XVI.

To Cranmer Henry went for aid,
   The wisest churchman of his realm;
To him his majesty portrayed
His love for Boleyn, peerless maid,
   And his own soul with doubts o'erwhelmed.

XVII.

Then Cranmer nobly did agree
   To ease his monarch's mind of trouble:
He bade him live rejoicingly,
Full soon he'd set him truly free
   From Catherine his most tiresome double.

XVIII.

Soon was the separation wrought,
   Catherine's heart was almost breaking;
The work was with rare triumph fraught,

For her who Henry's favor sought,
  In sooth, 'twas a grand undertaking.

XIX.

Queen Catherine, o'erwhelmed in woe,
  Besought her husband's love protection;
In vain the monarch bade her go,
To all her pleadings answered " No,"
  And plunged her soul in deep dejection.

XX.

To fill the measure of his sin,
  The Princess Mary from her mother
He ruthless tore; their suffering
He heeded not; most cruel king, ·
  He hated them and loved the *other*.

XXI.

The law was made, the deed was done,
  Henry with Boleyn was united;
Rejoicing in the prize he won,
He thought not of the hapless one,
  Whose life he had so sadly blighted.

XXII.

And in her far-off lone retreat,
  The *Queen* of England silent mourned,
She loved her husband, ('twas unmeet)
Aye, worshiped at his very feet,
  And at his call would have returned.

XXIII.

But he, o'erdazzled by the toy,

So bright and new and full of beauty,
Was happy, yes, without alloy
Of grief for her great was his joy
    To find in Anne love and duty.

XXIV.

At length one morn the tidings came,
    That Cather'ne was no more of mortals;
She died blessing King Henry's name,
Lauding his worth, his glory, fame,
    Till she had passed Death's shadowed portals

XXV.

When Henry heard the tidings sad,
    His heart relentless, grimly smote him,
All pleasures gay were grimly staid,
To mourn for Catherine all were bade,
    And while he grieved none dare approach him

XXVI.

All, all obeyed the king's behest,
    Save Anne, who in exultation,
Wore dress of white, she made the best
Of all her friends go gala dressed,
    "For now I'm queen of all the nation,"

XXVII.

This peerless lady gladly cried.
    Alas! for human pride and fashions,
Just three months later Anne died
Upon the block—so late a bride,
    The victim of her husband's passions,

XXVIII.

For faithlessness, so said the king,
  Who doomed his late won cherished idol;
Another bride he had in view,
Seymour fair, heart-free, tender, true,
  And Henry pan ed for the bridal.

XXIX.

Beneath a grand and stately oak,
  Poor An e's death toll Henry waited;
His robes were white, gayly he spoke
Of hounds and huntsmen, and evoked
  Much mirth, he being quite elated.

XXX.

At length the death-bells' solemn tones,
  Upon the air to him were borne,
Suggestive of poor Anne's groans,
Her stifled prayers and dying moans,
  When ruthless from her life was torn.

XXXI.

"Unleash the hounds," was his command,
  "To Seymour Castle let us turn,
To-morrow Lady Jane's fair hand
Will wear a bride's rich golden band,
  For faithless Anne none shall mourn."

XXXII.

The king brought home his new-made bride,
  He loved her with his heart's devotion;
But she erelong became his pride,

Gave him an heir, then calmly died,
  Thus in his favor won promotion.

XXXIII.

Poor Henry wept his loss awhile,
  But who can lead a life of mourning?
Full soon to love's sweet silver chime,
Our hero king was keeping time,
  And for another bride was yearning.

XXXIV.

The Duke of Cleves a sister had,
  A lady who loved ostentation,
And Henry though reputed bad
Among the ladies, she was glad
  To wed a d with him rule the nation.

XXXV.

But oh! alas for human taste,
  When Henry saw the willing maiden;
Her head and carriage, form and face,
Were void of beauty, aye, and grace,
  With plainness truly she was laden.

XXXVI.

Awhile heroically he bore,
  The dreadful task of toleration,
Then turned to Cranmer as before,
Who soon in twa n his *wedlock* tore,
  And sanctioned too their separation.

XXXVII.

After such vast experience,

One would dare fancy he was sated;
Not so; he spared neither expense
Nor e'en his royal influence,
    Till once again he had been mated.

XXXVIII.

This time he wooed and won a maid,
    Rarely, strange, surpassing beauty,
Who of her consort seemed afraid,
And near him ever staid,
    Nor lacked she in connubial duty.

XXXIX.

But Catherine Howard, heaven rest,
    Her soul was doomed in woe to perish;
Her husband cursed by fell unrest,
To still this demon in his breast,
    Condemned to death the wife he cherished.

XL.

For ANTE marriage faithlessness,
    So read poor Catherine's death warrant,
And Henry's fell bloodthirstiness,
Was sated by his victims thus,
    Until his name became abhorrent.

XLI.

Now surely none would risk their lives,
    By sharing Henry's crown and scepter;
Many were eager to be wives,
But then they'd wear the felon's jives,
    Rather than with the king sip nectar.

XLII.

Our hero hunted near and far,
   To find another would-be ruler;
At last he won a Mrs. Parr,
A widow beautiful and far
   More brave than soldier, aye, and cooler.

XLIII.

The new queen flattered all his whims,
   Deemed him more great than Alexander,
Knew that the name of wiser man,
Or one more brave since Time began,
   Was never in the world's calendar.

XLIV.

Yet, notwithstanding all her art,
   King Henry's minions plotted 'gainst her;
The king and queen they meant to part,
Against his bride he steeled his heart,
   And vowed he never would lament her.

XLV.

The order for the queen's arrest,
   Was issued by the cruel tyrant;
But when the soldiers Parr hard pressed,
She flew unto her husband's breast,
   And for his mercy was aspirant.

XLVI.

She wept and pleaded, coaxed and praised
   His wisdom, greatness, fame and glory,
And when the soldiers came he raised

His sword, with anger fairly blazed,
  And doomed them to the block so gory.

XLVII.

Well, Henry's days were nearly ran,
  His life of blood and crime was ending ;
But think ye of the hapless man,
When Death on him his work began,
  None dared to tell him what was pending.

XLVIII.

He died unwept, a thing of fear,
  None sighed o'er him in tender sorrow,
Forgotten were his virtues dear,
Remembered all his failings drear,
  The which the hardest heart would harrow.

XLIX.

But God, great Master of our lives,
  Had used the monster king in order,
To illustrate his ways most wise,
Change all not good unto his eyes,
  And lead us on to Heaven's bright border.

L.

The Reformation was the work,
  That Henry through his loves effected ;
In all his motives selfish lurked
Self-interest, nothing thus was shirked,
  But God's designs were all perfected.

THE END.